DEAD MAN'S BLUFF

Gabe shoved the extra six-gun behind his waist-band and latched onto Mace's boots. He dragged the corpse off the wagon and dumped it unceremoniously into the muddy, half-frozen street.

"I'm going to bring you down, Burr. I'm going to track and kill that two-toed bear and, when I do, I'll have all the answers to this reign of terror that you've used to empty this valley down to a handful of ranchers."

Burr began to shake with fury. "Mister, you're a walking dead man and you don't know it! I'll see that you're the one that's tracked down and killed like a rabid beast!"

SPECIAL PREVIEW

Turn to the back of this book for an exciting look at a classic epic trilogy . . .

Northwest Destiny

. . . the sprawling saga of brotherhood, pride and rage on the American frontier.

D1602736

Also in the LONG RIDER Series

LONG RIDER

★ MOUNTAIN KILLER ★

CLAY DAWSON

DIAMOND BOOKS, NEW YORK

This book is a Diamond original edition, and has never
been previously published.

MOUNTAIN KILLER

A Diamond Book / published by arrangement with
the author

PRINTING HISTORY
Diamond edition / September 1992

ISBN: 1-55773-773-8

Diamond Books are published by The Berkley Publishing Group,
200 Madison Avenue, New York, New York 10016.
The name "DIAMOND" and its logo are trademarks
belonging to Charter Communications, Inc.

PRINTED IN THE UNITED STATES OF AMERICA

10 9 8 7 6 5 4 3 2 1

CHAPTER ONE

It was autumn, and there was a sharp bite to the cold Rocky Mountain air when Long Rider rolled out of his blankets. To the east, the first rays of sunlight lanced over the Sangre de Cristo Mountains and penetrated clouds already beginning to turn salmon. There was a thin sheet of ice across the swift stream not far from where Gabe Conrad had made his Spartan camp. Nearby his horse stamped its hooves in an effort to stay warm.

Gabe rubbed the circulation back into his hands and quickly pulled on his moccasins, then the heavy, buffalo hide coat with the faint yellow image of the Thunderbird. Years earlier, Gabe, known as Long Rider among the Oglala Sioux, had cut the shredded remains of his mother's tepee and then sewn the buffalo hide into a coat. His mother, like many other women and children, had died in a dawn cavalry attack upon their peaceful Sioux village.

In the nearby pines, a blue jay raucously scolded a squirrel. Gabe surveyed the forest and sky thinking that this would be another beautiful October day, but that he sure wouldn't want to be up in this high country two months from now when the snow was higher than a tepee top. Gabe had been raised near the Black Hills of the Dakotas and was accustomed to the Plains, but he had discovered that these Rocky Mountains were very much to his liking. He enjoyed the rugged panoramas and the sharp, invigorating scent of pine.

Gabe moved over to his rifle and stood very still for several minutes as he judged the direction of the morning breeze. Satisfied that he would be downwind of the canyon where he would hunt deer, Gabe left his camp and started for the canyon being especially careful to avoid stepping in the places where leaves lay brittle and ready to crackle a warning.

Gabe was a white man, but having been raised by the Oglala until age fifteen, he was a skilled and stealthy hunter. His lean, athletic body soon warmed up to his hard exertion, and his eyes and ears were alert for game. He had not had fresh venison in nearly four days, subsisting instead on trout, sage hens, and a couple of fat rabbits.

The canyon he followed was choked with brush and trees, but Gabe was sure it was also a rich source of deer and possibly even elk. He saw their spoor and felt confident that, if he could only get a clear shot, he would be roasting venison steaks in less than an hour. He would gorge himself, then make enough jerky to carry him down to Old Santa Fe where he intended to winter.

Gabe approached a rushing stream and studied the patches of mud between the rocks and saw the tracks of many deer. He could feel their presence but knew that the heavy growth in the canyon was going to make accurate shooting very difficult. He decided that he would move back from the stream and wait until a buck or doe came in to drink and then he would have his meat.

Gabe stepped lightly from rock to rock, wanting to avoid stepping on the dried leaves at all costs. Crouching and moving without a sound, he entered a thick stand of aspen, hunkered down with a clear view of the stream, and waited.

Ten minutes passed with the only sound in his ears that of the rushing stream. The canyon was very cold, and Gabe kept rubbing his hands together to keep them warm. Come on, he thought, it's time for breakfast.

He was just about to consider moving upstream when suddenly a sixth sense born of a lifetime of living in the wilderness told him that something was very wrong. The birds in the branches overhead had stopped their chirruping, and the stillness caused the hairs on Gabe's neck to stand up straight.

Gabe spun around as he heard a crashing of underbrush so near and so loud that it could only be the charge of a grizzly bear. His Winchester slammed to his shoulder, and even before he saw the huge bear, Gabe began firing the weapon with both speed and precision.

The grizzly was on him in an instant. His bullets had struck the huge bear three times, but none of the slugs had penetrated a vital organ. One shot had actually glanced off the massive skull and blown away the beast's right ear.

Enraged, the grizzly slapped Gabe's rifle aside. Gabe's hand flashed to the gun on his hip, but the bear's immense paw crashed into his left shoulder and knocked the pistol loose, sending Gabe flying. He landed ten feet away on his backside in the ice-crusted stream with no rifle or pistol for defense.

The grizzly stood up on its hind legs and roared. Gabe saw that the huge creature was bleeding heavily and one of his rifle slugs even appeared to have penetrated its chest, but the .44-40 slug lacked enough of a wallop to knock the animal down, and now Gabe found himself on his back in freezing water with a some of his own meat torn from his left shoulder.

Challenge made, the grizzly dropped to all fours and charged. Gabe yanked a bowie knife from the sheath under his coat and scrambled to his feet. He ducked a ponderous swipe by the grizzly that would have decapitated him and drove his long and heavy blade into the bear's side, just under its ribs.

The grizzly screamed like a gut-shot horse and staggered as Gabe slammed his steel in once more. Gabe then escaped a whistling blow and scrambled up the bank in a desperate search for his six-gun. He kept his knife clenched in his bloody fist as a last resort.

The six-gun was lying in plain sight, and he snatched it up as the roaring grizzly lunged up the bank and threw itself on him in demented fury. Gabe unleased three bullets into its head, and when the bear tried to clamp its massive jaws on his throat, he buried his blade into the grizzly's throat. Warm blood flooded across his chest as the bear collapsed in death.

Gabe rolled the huge beast away and crawled back down to the mountain stream. He scooped up a handful of broken ice and rubbed it across his wounds in an effort to stop the bleeding. The ice not only quenched the flow of blood, it also numbed his pain and Gabe was able to see that his wounds, while not mortal, were serious enough to require the attention of a good doctor.

Gabe climbed unsteadily to his feet. He'd been told that there was a ranching, logging, and mining settlement not more than twenty miles to the southwest called Mesa. Perhaps Mesa would have a doctor or at least someone who would sew up his shoulder.

Gabe was shivering and his lips were blue from cold when he finally reached his camp. He piled the last of his wood on the campfire and used a smoke-blackened coffeepot to boil water. For the next half hour, he tried to clean his wounds and then bind them tight with strips torn from his extra shirt. It was awkward, and he wasn't a bit satisfied with his efforts. Finally he thought, the hell with it, and dragged his saddle over to his horse.

Because Gabe was covered with his own blood as well as that of the grizzly, his buckskin gelding snorted and pulled back with fear.

"Easy," Long Rider said, clenching his teeth with pain as he tried to calm the spooky animal. "I want to get out of here just as bad as you do. So just simmer down and I'll get this damn saddle blanket straight and my saddle cinched down tight. Let me do that and we'll be on our way in no time at all."

His soothing voice calmed the buckskin, and Gabe bridled then one-armed his forty-pound saddle in place. He glanced at his shoulder, and saw that it was bleeding again, and figured there was no sense wasting any more time in trying to tighten the bandages. The most important thing was to get some help before the loss of blood made him weak. This was a hard country for a badly wounded man to travel alone.

Gabe had some trouble tightening his cinch with one hand because the fingers of his left hand would not work smoothly. "The hell with it," he said, figuring that he could live with the cinch somewhat looser than he'd have liked.

Packing his gear into a heavy canvas duffle and tying it down took only a few minutes, but the effort left him feeling dizzy and he knew that it was due to the loss of blood. If he were among his own people, a medicine man would brew up some bark and herbs to make a steaming poultice. The poultice would be slapped on his torn shoulder hot enough to scald the skin and make him break out in a cold sweat, but it would also draw out the poisons left by the grizzly's claws. In three, maybe four days, the wound would be healing up nice and, in a month, he'd be fit again.

Gabe smothered his fire, mounted his horse, and headed out at a gallop. He looked up at the rising sun, seeing a blurry orange and red orb, and he hoped to hell that he'd reach Mesa before he lost consciousness.

CHAPTER TWO

The buckskin gelding seemed to realize that its master's strength was bleeding away. The animal galloped until it was winded and lathered before slowing to a walk as Gabe swayed in the saddle. About noon, the gelding found a well-worn trail and followed it for several hours before it brought Gabe to the edge of a huge valley.

Gabe raised his head and tried to focus on a log cabin, corrals, and shop just about a mile ahead. He thought he could see smoke trailing from the chimney of the cabin, but the corrals were empty, and he saw neither dogs, sheep, cows, or horses. Pushing himself erect against the saddle horn and feeling his left shoulder throb, he touched the heels of his moccasins to the gelding's flanks and rode out of the forest, the sun warming a body that had grown cold. His eyelids were drooping heavily and it was taking all his strength just to stay awake when his horse suddenly spun out from under him in fright and Gabe pitched to the meadow beside the rotting, half-buried corpse of a dead cow.

Gabe momentarily lost consciousness but then roused himself enough to scoot away from the cow, noting that its exposed skull had deep claw marks that could only have been left by a grizzly. He managed to climb to his feet and stagger over to his horse which had stopped to graze only about twenty yards away.

"Easy," he said, grabbing the animal's reins. The buckskin snorted in fear, and Gabe drew his Winchester from his saddle scabbard, wondering if yet another grizzly was close by and if he was about to be attacked a second time. But the forest remained still and dark, so Gabe struggled back into the saddle and rode the last few hundred yards up before the small ranch.

"Hello the house!" he shouted.

There was no answer. Gabe sighed with disappointment. His gray eyes scanned the huge valley that doglegged to the west following a river. This immense, high-mountain valley was a good twenty miles wide and he could not tell how long. Gabe saw tiny dots that he was sure were cattle. There was enough grass for thousands of cattle and the surrounding peaks offered good protection from blizzards and deep snow.

Gabe looked back to the cabin. He knew he hadn't enough strength left to ride on. If he lost consciousness and fell into the tall, brown meadow grass, he might bleed to death before he was found.

"End of the line," he said as he unloaded from the buckskin, almost toppling into the yard. He stood hanging onto his saddle for several minutes, mustering up his strength before he took a few wobbly steps to the heavy pine door. Incredibly, he saw more claw marks cut deeply into the wood.

What the devil kind of a valley was this—a paradise for killer grizzly? Gabe pushed open the door to the cabin and stumbled inside. The shaft of light from the doorway revealed a tidy, one room cabin with a plank floor and a good stove with a dying fire and serviceable but rough-hewn log furniture. There were two plates of cold food on the table served but uneaten giving the cabin the appearance of a hasty desertion.

Gabe lurched over to the log table and sat down heavily. The plates were laden with hunks of pork laying in congealed fat surrounded by corn dodgers. There were also two cups of cold black coffee.

"Ain't no sense in letting good food go to waste," Gabe said, knowing that he had to eat something before he rested and tried to recover his strength.

He emptied the plates using his fingers and gulped down the coffee as well. Then, he managed to get back on his feet and weave across the room to a double bed where he collapsed. The bed was as soft as goose down, and Gabe closed his eyes. He wasn't going any farther this day. The good news was that the bleeding had stopped, but the bad news was that his claw-torn shoulder was almost certain to suppurate with infection.

It could not be helped. Gabe had played out his string as far as it would go and now he had to sleep. If he was lucky, help would arrive and maybe someone would be kind enough to load him in a buckboard and deliver him to a doctor. It was the best that he could hope for.

When Ella Porter saw the saddled buckskin horse grazing in the meadow near her open door, she reined in her rickety buckboard and snatched up a rifle that had been resting at her side. The rifle was old and single-shot, but it packed a heavy .50 caliber slug, one plenty big enough to knock down a charging grizzly or open a fist-size hole through an outlaw's chest.

Ella tied the lines around the brake of the buckboard, jumped down, and hunkered down behind the wagon. Having just returned from the cemetery at Mesa where her husband had been buried this very morning, Ella felt hollow inside. Her eyes were red and puffy, but her hands were steady on the rifle. She'd be damned if some drifter was going to catch her with her guard down just because she no longer had a husband for protection.

She rested the big rifle across the wagon bed and made sure it was ready to fire before she took a deep breath and called, "Come on out of there, whoever you are!"

There was no answer. The leggy buckskin gelding raised its head and whinnied to her own dapple mare, but then it returned to grazing.

"Mister, I got a buffalo rifle trained on that doorway and I got neighbors who'll come help me so you'd better just come out with your hands up and then be on your way. If you've eaten at my table, I won't kill you for it, but you sure aren't welcome to stay."

A tendril of honey-blond hair slipped down over her eyes and Ella curled her tongue and blew it away. She waited . . . and waited.

"Dammit, mister, I said come on out!"

The minutes dragged by, and when Ella could stand it no longer, she swore and kicked the wheel of her wagon in frustration. What the hell was she going to do now? No doubt some sneaky polecat was waiting in the shadows inside her cabin with his own rifle, and the minute she showed herself, she'd either be shot or allowed to go inside the cabin where the man would overpower her and then have his wicked way with her.

Ella wiped a thin sheen of nervous perspiration from her forehead with her sleeve. She knew that she ought to just lead her dapple mare out of rifle range and drive off to get help from her nearest neighbor. But John Paxton's ranch was nearly eight miles up the valley, and Ella simply wanted to return to her cabin and be allowed to mourn the loss of her husband in peace.

"Damn you!" Ella screamed in frustration. "Mister, I lost my husband to a killer grizzly bear night before last and I don't need no more trouble. Please! Just come on out and ride away!"

Ella discovered that her cheeks were wet and she was crying. She wiped her face dry with her sleeve and stood up with the rifle. To hell with it, she thought angrily. Whoever is inside will have to kill me before I kill him.

With the heavy rifle clenched in her hands, Ella marched toward her cabin expecting to be shot at any moment. But when she passed near the grazing buckskin, she saw how its saddle was covered with black, caked blood.

Ella lowered her rifle and moved quickly to the horse. Yes, it was blood. She turned and dropped her rifle, then hurried into her cabin to find Long Rider asleep in her bed. The interior of her cabin was dim, but not so dim that Ella could not see the dark, bulky bandage that covered the sleeping man's left shoulder. She knelt by the bed and reached for Gabe's pulse. He did not stir as she felt for his heartbeat. When she found his pulse, she was relieved that it was steady, but not strong.

Ella hurried outside to her woodpile and came in with an armful of firewood. Feeding the stove, she got water to boil and then she located one of her husband's shirts and ripped it into bandaging strips. When the water was hot, she carried the kettle over to her bedside and then used the stranger's own blood-caked knife to cut away his shirt.

"Grizzly!" she whispered, staring at the same kind of horrible claw marks that she had found on her husband's body less than forty-eight hours earlier. Actually, her husband's wounds had not been as unsightly, but the grizzly had apparently broken his neck because there had been a dark bruise at the base of his skull. At least poor Edgar had died suddenly; he hadn't been eaten alive like all the cattle and horses they'd lost to the hated grizzlies.

Gabe's eyes flew open as Ella began to clean his shoulder. For a moment, he struggled and one of his big fists lashed out at the young woman, but she had been expecting a startled reaction and managed to avoid getting knocked to the floor.

"Easy, mister! I don't mean to hurt you."

"Who . . . who are you?"

"I'm the one that owns this ranch. Who are you?"

"Gabe Conrad. I had a run-in with a grizzly." Gabe closed his eyes and opened them again to make sure that they were not playing tricks on him. "Why are you all dressed in black?"

"My husband also had a bear fight," Ella explained quietly, "only in his case, the bear broke his neck two days ago. So I'm in mourning."

Gabe rolled his head back and forth on his pillow and stared up at the cabin's roof as her words slowly penetrated his mind. "How come . . ."

"Maybe you better just hold the questions until later," Ella said in a small voice. "You aren't fit for talking, and I don't much feel up to it either. I'll just say that you have entered los Osos Valley, 'the Valley of the Bears,' and those of us that have been trying to ranch up here have been fighting for our lives and our livestock for some time now. And in my case, I've lost the fight."

Gabe understood. Grizzly had always been the bane of his people and of the early mountain men. Indian legends spoke of a time when the ferocious grizzly roamed unopposed in the mountains. They killed men who entered their domain and were vulnerable only when they left the forest and ventured out onto the plains where they could be overtaken by mounted warriors. Without the protection of the forest, Indian warriors could surround and bring down the grizzly with spears and arrows. And so it had been between the Indian and the grizzly since the introduction of the horse by the Spaniards centuries earlier—the ferocious bears reigning supreme in the forests, the warriors the masters of the plains.

"This valley has always been cursed by the grizzly," Ella said. "The Spaniards tried to use its grass to fatten their horses but found their muskets no match against the bears. Nothing has changed. We are trying to ranch here, but the bears keep killing our livestock, and sometimes even our men."

"I am sorry about your husband."

For a moment, grief swept over Ella so powerfully that her words were barely a whisper as she cleaned Long Rider's mauled shoulder. "This valley has the finest mountain-meadow grass in the world. Livestock fatten on it like they were eating sugarcane. We got ready markets in Denver City and Old Santa Fe. We can sell all the cattle and sheep we can deliver, but the grizzly just won't let us be."

"Why don't the ranchers get together with dogs and hunt the grizzly out?"

"They've tried without luck. Dogs get killed or wind up missing in the heavy forest. Even worse, ranchers like my husband have discovered the tracks of a killer bear and go off to hunt it down and they simply vanish."

Ella let Long Rider digest her words a moment then said, "Mister, would you be interested in hunting out our grizzly if the money was right?"

"I'm sorry ma'am. I've killed a few bear in my time, and the one that tore up my shoulder was about as big and ornery as they come, but I don't want any more of that for any amount of money. Besides, I plan to winter in Santa Fe."

"I can't say as I blame you," Ella said, unable to hide her disappointment.

"Listen," Gabe offered, "when I reach Santa Fe, I'll ask about. With any luck at all, I can find several good bounty hunters who'd be willing to come up here next spring with dogs and solve your bear problem."

"I'll probably have to sell out before then. I've less than two hundred head of cattle and, without my husband, there's no way that I can stay here all winter. Not alone, I can't."

"Maybe you can get a fair price for your spread and do better in a town somewhere," Gabe said, marveling at how gently the woman's fingers touched his torn flesh. "Even without the grizzly, the winters have got to be pretty hard up here and ranching is never easy. If the grass is as good as you claim, I'm sure you can get a decent price for your ranch."

"Not a chance," she told him.

"Why not?"

"Because there's a man named Caleb Burr that lives on the other end of this valley. And although he started out just like the rest of us, he's prospered. His herds number several thousand."

"So why don't the grizzly give him the same fits they're giving you?"

"I guess they don't like the north end of the valley as well. It's a little more exposed to the wind and the snow gets deeper in the winter. Even so, I'm sure Caleb loses a few head each year to grizzly and wolves, but nothing like us small ranchers."

"I see," Gabe said, not seeing at all. "How many are there of you?"

"Five families is all that's left. We used to have almost a dozen scattered from one end of the valley to the other. But

Caleb bought them off, and now he even owns the sawmill and the local mine."

"Sounds like he's got things his own way," Gabe said, noting anger and bitterness in the young widow's voice.

"That he does," Ella said, "and I expect, if things keep going as they are, he'll own all of los Osos Valley in the next year or two. Then, instead of it being a place where people can make a strong ranching community, it'll be nothing more than one man's company town."

Gabe was silent for quite some time before he said, "It's too bad that you folks didn't hire some real good mountain men to come in and hunt those grizzly out for a bounty. There are men that will do it, you know. Most of them are savvy old-timers." For a moment he fondly recalled his old friend, Jim Bridger.

"We tried to hire a few. They disappeared in the mountains and were never seen again. After the word got out about them, we couldn't hire hunters at any price. It was as if this valley became hexed."

Gabe closed his eyes. "Getting mauled or eaten by a thousand-pound grizzly sure isn't something a man likes to think about."

"You need a doctor to sew this shoulder up," Ella said, "but there isn't one in Mesa."

Gabe opened his eyes. "So who sews folks up when they get hurt?"

"Whoever is closest and sober."

"Then get yourself a needle and thread, ma'am, and I'll pay you for the trouble."

"I'll take no pay," she told him, "not for mending a body torn by an animal."

Gabe watched the woman go find a needle and thread. He noticed that she moved with a weariness beyond her years, and Gabe had the strong impression that life in los

Osos Valley had been a constant nightmare because of
the fierce grizzly. No one needed to tell Gabe just how
intelligent and cunning those beasts could be when stalking
man or livestock. A grizzly could move through the thickets
as quiet as a mouse when he hunted, and when he charged,
he could sprint like a puma.

Gabe knew as well as anyone that, when a man stood
face to face with a charging grizzly, the biggest rifle ever
made was useless if the shooter did not place his bullets in
one of the grizzly's few vital spots. Knowing those spots
was one thing, having the nerve to stand up to a grizzly's
charge was quite another, and many a man, red and white,
had panicked and lost his life in a moment of bloody horror.
If Gabe never saw another grizzly in his entire life, it would
not be too soon.

"This is going to hurt," Ella warned as she threaded the
needle with heavy twine. "My husband has some whiskey
in the cabinet, I'll get it and—"

"Never mind the whiskey," Gabe said. "I don't drink hard
liquor."

She blinked with surprise. "What are you, a preacher or
something?"

"No, ma'am. I was raised by the Oglala Sioux, and I've
seen too many of those people destroyed by the white man's
whiskey. It makes strong men weak and weak men think
they're strong. Either way, it's bad."

Ella studied Long Rider's face, thinking he was a very
handsome man, darkly tanned by the sun. She noted his
right index finger and how it was broken and twisted at a
sharp angle. There was probably an interesting story behind
that she thought.

"Grab ahold of the bed frame."

Gabe did as he was told and when he felt the needle
enter his flesh, his body stiffened but otherwise displayed

no outward indication of the pain. He even watched Ella as she stitched up the wound, neat and quick. Her hands were callused from hard work, like the hands of all frontier women and Indian squaws. You could find men who had soft hands on the frontier, gamblers, slackers, and gunmen were a few—but you'd never come across an Indian woman or a rancher or a homesteader's wife who didn't have rough, chapped hands.

"Where will you be going after you sell the ranch?" he asked when Ella was finished sewing and patching him up as good as most any doctor or tooth-yanker.

"I'm not sure that I will sell."

"But I thought you said that you couldn't make it through the coming winter without a man."

"I did say that, didn't I?" Ella rose stiffly to her feet and went to stoke the fire. "Well, maybe I'll just have to find another good one."

The way she said it might have sounded hard to some considering that she'd just buried her husband. But Gabe admired a practical woman, and this one would quite obviously take a stand and fight for what she wanted. Ella was also damned pretty, pretty enough to attract any number of bachelors—even in los Osos Valley.

"I expect I'll be leaving tomorrow," Gabe said. "I'd not want to cause you any embarrassment."

"Embarrassment doesn't concern me anymore. I don't much care what people say. You were hurt; I was willing and plenty able to help. That is the way a Christian is supposed to think and act."

When she was finished rebandaging his wound, Ella said, "I can't say how clean your shoulder will heal. It might be ugly for a while, but I think we can keep it from turning black with gangrene if we keep it clean."

"That's not your problem," Gabe replied, "because, like

I said, I'll be moving along."

"Suit yourself," Ella told him as she went to the cabinet, found a bottle and poured herself three fingers of whiskey which she downed in a gulp.

Gabe came to his feet and went outside to unsaddle his horse. "Mind if we put up in the barn with that dapple mare?" he asked, poking his head back inside. "The weather looks like it's brewin' up a storm tonight."

"You can sleep in here on the floor," she told him.

"Are you sure?"

"Of course I am! If you try any funny business, I'll punch you in the shoulder and that will turn your mind serious."

Gabe had to chuckle. "You're right about that," he said agreeably.

Ella pulled on a heavy sheepskin coat and went outside to help him get the horses into the barn which had a hayloft packed with cut grass.

"That's a lot of hay you got put up," Gabe said.

"If the winter isn't too bad, it'll get what few cattle I have left through the winter," Ella said. "Used to be we had two barns this size and could winter about seven hundred head. We hired men each year to cut and put up the hay, but the barns burned down one year and we never had the money to replace them."

"How'd they fire?"

"No one knows for certain," Ella said, her mouth twisting in anger, "but I've got my suspicion that it was Caleb Burr. That man has been trying to buy us out for years, but we won't sell."

Gabe unsaddled his horse and turned it into a stall. He went outside and glanced up at the dark storm clouds piling up over the Sangre de Cristo Mountains. "You reckon it'll snow?"

"Not yet," Ella said. "But give it another month and we'll

have some. Still, this valley is protected from the worst storms by the surrounding mountains. That's what makes it so attractive."

"To men," Gabe said, "and also to grizzly."

Ella nodded and helped him unhitch the dapple mare, then lead her inside. She found a fork and used it to pitch hay to both horses. Gabe's buckskin went at the dried grass like it was candy.

"That horse of yours needs about a hundred pounds more on his bones to survive up in this country."

"He's tough," Gabe said, "and he'll winter fine in Santa Fe."

Ella set the pitchfork aside and helped Gabe untie his duffle bag. "Where you from?" she asked.

"Black Hills country."

"Any special reason why you *have* to winter in Santa Fe?"

"Nope, I guess not. I just figure that I could find work there and the climate is to my liking."

"You could find work here."

"No, ma'am. I'm not interested in hunting grizzly."

Ella looked him straight in the eye. "Why not? You afraid of them?"

Gabe had to smile. "Any man *not* afraid of them would be a fool. But that isn't it. The Indians believe that the bear is strong medicine. We always have. Hunting them is not an idea to my liking."

"But you killed one just yesterday and almost got yourself killed, so—"

"I killed that bear to save my own hide," Gabe explained, "but I'm not fond enough of money to go killing them off for a bounty."

Ella sighed. "I don't understand your thinking, but I respect your right to make your own choices. Even so,

I don't think you'll be ready to ride out of here in the morning."

"We'll see," Gabe told her, wondering what would happen to this strong but stubborn woman if she decided to remain in los Osos Valley.

CHAPTER THREE

A violent, high-country storm broke over los Osos Valley about midnight. Gabe awoke to the sound of heavy rolling thunder and the sight of lightning bolts striking the earth so close and with such force that he could feel the cabin shake.

Before they'd gone to bed, Ella had tacked a blanket up between them so that she could change out of her dress of mourning into a long, woolen nightshirt. Now she was also wide awake.

"Just listen to it!" she whispered, coming to her feet and tiptoeing over to the window to stare out at the brilliant lightning flashes and the pouring rain.

Gabe did not get up, but from his angle on the floor, he could see plenty of fireworks, too. He'd always heard that the Rockies had some pretty big thunder and lightning storms, and now he was a believer.

"I'm mighty glad that I'm not sleeping outside on the ground this night," he said, "because it sure would be miserable."

Ella turned toward him as another flash of lightning made her features glow. "My late husband, Mr. Edgar Porter, God rest his soul, was a good man. He was twenty years older than I. When we were first married, I was just fifteen, and I called him Daddy. He could build a watertight roof on four solid walls and was good with cattle and horses. Are you?"

Gabe started. "Beg your pardon, ma'am?"

"I asked if you're good with cattle and horses?"

"Well, I've forked a few broncs and ridden the rough string. I like horses. But as for cattle, I've worked on a ranch or two, but I sure don't consider myself a cowboy."

"Can your rope?"

Gabe chuckled. "How come you're asking me all these questions in the middle of the night?"

"I was curious, Gabe, that's all. How does your shoulder feel?"

"It's felt better."

"I shouldn't doubt it," Ella said, turning away from the window and then stoking the fire. "At least it's your left arm. You are right-handed, aren't you?"

"I am."

"But you wear your gun handle forward on your right hip." The lady's voice left no doubt she was asking a question.

"I use a cross draw," Gabe explained.

"Because of that twisted finger?"

Gabe pushed himself up into a sitting position. It appeared that the woman wanted to talk more than sleep. "Yes," he said, "though I've also trained myself to use a gun with either hand."

"Are you fast?"

In Gabe's Indian culture, modesty and generosity were the most highly esteemed qualities among men and women alike, so he answered, "There are probably slower and faster men on the draw, but I generally hit what I aim for."

"I'll just bet you do."

Ella was silent for a couple of minutes. Just when Gabe was about to lie back down and go to sleep, the woman said, "My husband and I own six thousand deeded acres of this fine valley. We own more than any of the others and have some of the best stands of timber in all of Colorado. That alone is worth a lot of money to a logging man."

"Then you should sell your timber to one if you need the money," Gabe said, trying not to yawn.

"But I don't want to sell! No one will give me anything approaching a fair price."

"Then *don't* sell," Gabe said, with increasing exasperation. "Do whatever you please, ma'am."

"Call me Ella," she snapped. "You sure aren't a very talkative man, are you, Mr. Conrad?"

"Not in the middle of the night," he told her. "Night is for sleepin' or . . . well, it's not for talking."

Ella sniffled. "I'm going to miss poor Edgar. He was a real peach. Oh, he had his faults. He didn't like to bath or shave, and he ate like a wild beast after its kill. His teeth were mostly gone, and he spit tobacco juice on the floor— some bad habits you can't ever cure—but he was kind and affectionate."

That wasn't difficult for Gabe to imagine. Edgar sounded like an old reprobate that had gotten lucky enough to marry a real beauty about half his age. No wonder the old goat had been affectionate.

Ella was saying, "In his own fashion, Edgar was a man who could make money. For instance, two years ago, he found a little gold in some stream less than two days ride from here. He never would tell anybody where the damned stream was—not even me! But I got a fair idea. It was the gold he panned that gave him enough money to buy us this valley land free and clear."

When Gabe did not make a comment, Ella said, "You ever prospected for gold?"

"No."

"It's to be found up here, Gabe. I followed Edgar's tracks almost to the spot one time before I lost them in a river. But I got a strong suspicion I could find that gold he was working. Might be I could help you find a little yourself, but only if you were to forget about traveling on down to Santa Fe."

Gabe sat up stiffly. "Listen," he said with more than a little asperity, "if you have some kind of proposition, why don't you just spit it out and be done with it so we can both get some sleep?"

"You're upset because your shoulder is bothering you," she told him. "Anyone would be. You're in pain and—"

"And I like to sleep at night," he interrupted in a terse voice. "So whatever it is you want to say, say it, or let me sleep."

"You're a blunt-speaking man, aren't you?" Ella said, brushing back her long, honey-blond hair and wiping a tear from her eye.

"In the middle of the night, I am."

Gabe heard her sniffle and was stabbed with guilt. After all, the woman had doctored, fed, and given him a dry place to sleep, not to mention putting his horse up in a solid barn with her precious winter hay.

"Ma'am," he said, "I apologize for being so short. I am normally as easygoing a fella as you'll ever want to meet, but I guess this day was sort of a tough one, and I'm a little out of sorts. That, however, is no excuse to be rude to a lady. So I do apologize."

Ella drew up a chair beside the stove and waved her hand in a gesture of dismissal to let him know that his apology was accepted. "Gabe, I *do* have something I can't wait to discuss. And even though you refuse to hunt the grizzly that are wiping me and my neighbors out, I won't hold that against you."

"Thanks."

"But," she added quickly, "I am sort of in a fix."

"I can see that you are," he told her. "A woman up here with a big ranch to run and no husband. But you'll find a good man and—"

"Maybe *you're* the good man I need."

"Oh no!" Gabe shook his head. "Now listen here, I am not a cowboy, and I have no interest in settling down to ranching."

"Not even if I gave you part interest in the ranch?"

"Not even," he said.

"Or if I helped you to find some gold next spring?"

"By next spring, I figure to be in Arizona Territory poking around."

Ella scowled. "But I need some help this winter!"

"Then ride along with me into Mesa and hire it," Gabe said. "And if you're without cash, then trade a few cows or promises for it. You'll have plenty of willing takers. What you're offering is the chance that most men dream about."

"You don't understand anything," Ella told him. "You see, there's no one in this whole wide valley that will oppose Caleb Burr and his riders. He'd run them out of here . . ."

Ella fell silent, aware that she'd said much more than she'd planned.

Gabe frowned. "So that's it. You need a man-killer as well as a grizzly-killer, and I appear to be both."

"Well, not yet you don't," she said. "Not with that shoulder. But in a few weeks . . ."

"No," he said flatly, as he lay back down and squeezed his eyes shut. "The answer is just . . . no! I'm going to

Santa Fe tomorrow, and that's the end of it."

"Well, besides looking for a job—which I've already offered you—what's so damned important for you to do in Santa Fe?"

Gabe didn't really have an answer. He didn't know anyone in Santa Fe, but he'd just decided he'd like to see that historic old crossroads town and spend the winter there if he found it to his liking.

"Good night, Mrs. Porter," he told her, pulling his blankets up to his chin even though the woman had stoked the fire up so high that he was breaking into a sweat.

She snapped back something, but her words were drowned out by the lightning. Maybe it was just as well. Ella was pretty damned mad, and the night wasn't getting any younger.

In the morning, he awoke to the delicious smell of coffee brewing and pork frying in a skillet.

"Would you like some fried potatoes along with the pork?" she asked him with a smile.

Gabe knuckled the sleep from his eyes. "Sure," he said, hearing his belly rumble.

"Then best get yourself up and washed."

Gabe stood up slowly. He had gone to sleep fully dressed and now he tucked his shirttails into his pants and inspected Ella's bandaging with approval. "Looks like it's scabbed over and on the mend."

"We'll see after breakfast," she told him. "The storm passed and it's going to be a fine day. We need to check on the cattle and then I got some—"

"Whoa up there!" Gabe said. "I thought I explained things last night about leaving today for New Mexico."

Ella stopped forking the pork around and regarded him with a smile that did not quite work. "Thought you might realize that I've got something here for you that you won't find anyplace else. Something much better. I got a feeling we could make a good team."

"Maybe we could," Gabe said, not wanting to sound abrupt, "but I'm just not ready to settle down. Not even for a chance to own part of a ranch and find some gold."

Ella shook her head. "It's just got to be the Indian in you that's messed up your thinking," she said. "Any right-thinking man would jump at the chance I'm offering."

"Well," Gabe told her, "I never did claim to be the smartest drifter in the West. But I do aim to go where I want when I want, and I like things pretty much changing all the time. I'm just not a settlin' down kind of man."

"You might be," Ella said, forking the meat out of her skillet and pouring Gabe a cup of coffee, "if you ever gave it a fair try. You see, teamed up with the right kind of man, I could pull this valley back together and hold off Caleb Burr and his boys."

"Maybe you should offer this Caleb fella what you offered me?" Gabe said.

Ella snorted with derision. "He's as ugly as a boar hog and just as greedy and mean when he has you under his thumb. I couldn't stand the sight, much less the touch of him."

Well, Gabe thought, that settles that idea. Ella Porter sure did sound definite about her feelings toward the big, north-end rancher.

"I hope you don't hold it against me that I mean to travel on."

Ella shook her head and her mouth crimped down at the corners. It was plain that she was greatly disappointed by his lack of interest in her proposal, but Gabe figured that the poor woman was probably still a little in shock over the loss of her husband and not yet thinking clearly. Grief could do that to anybody. And while some women who'd just lost their husbands might shy away from any man for a good long while, perhaps others would grab any man at all out of sheer desperation. Ella, it seemed, was of the latter type.

"I'd best be on my way after breakfast. I'd like to pay you something for—"

"No!"

The way she said it left no doubt in Gabe's mind that arguing would be a waste of his breath and probably make her even more upset, so he took his place at the table. Ella poured him coffee, then fed him. They ate together in silence. It wasn't until he was fidgeting and ready to go out and saddle his horse that she said, "I need some supplies in Mesa. Might as well ride along together, huh?"

She wouldn't meet his eyes, so great was her disappointment, and Gabe did not have the heart to tell her that he'd about as soon ride alone. She was a mighty fine-looking widow, even with her eyes ringed with dark circles that told him she had not slept well and that her husband's death was a great loss.

"Sure," he said. "I'll hitch up the mare, saddle my buckskin, and we can be on our way."

Gabe pushed himself to his feet and reached for his hat. "I thank you for the meal."

"I should check on that wound."

"It'll be fine," he said. "Santa Fe ought to be less than a hundred miles south of here. When I get there, I can have it examined by a doctor."

"You watch out," she said. "Some doctors are just quacks trying to peddle their own brand of snake oil and elixir."

"I'll make sure that I find an honest one," he said, pulling on his coat and going out the door to take care of the horses.

Ella stayed inside until the buckboard was hitched and the gelding was saddled. Then she came out of her cabin dressed in a man's coat, pants, and shirt. She was wearing a pair of old, high-topped cowboy boots, and with her pretty hair shoved up under her husband's slouch hat, she looked like a boy instead of a full-breasted woman in her mid-twenties.

Without a word of greeting, Ella hopped up into the wagon seat and took the lines. She slapped them rather sharply across the dapple mare's rump, and the animal jumped forward in its harness so suddenly that Ella almost spilled over the back of her seat.

Gabe had to hurry to mount his buckskin and catch up with her and, when he did, he stepped off his horse into the buckboard and said, "I think I'd better drive, Mrs. Porter."

Ella did not argue as she handed Gabe the reins, her eyes as bleak as yesterday's sky.

The way to Mesa was north and Gabe was riding south to Santa Fe, but the woman seemed to need his company and he owed her too much to bring up the fact that he was riding out of his way.

"It's a fine morning," he said, noting how the rain had washed the sky a pretty, bright blue and how the pine trees that bordered the valley were glistening with raindrops. "Nothing finer than a morning after a rain, is there?"

Ella said nothing. She looked upset and acted preoccupied. Gabe decided that it would not help to try to cheer her up because Ella was just too bogged down by the weight of her considerable troubles.

Mesa, as it turned out, was bigger than Gabe had expected. There were two saloons, no church or schoolhouse, but a half dozen hotels, a sawmill on the river that spewed smoke into the air, and several busy stores selling supplies and equipment. As they entered the main street of town, Gabe noted that Mesa could boast a livery, gunsmith, and saddle shops.

"Interesting town," he said, observing how burly logging men mingled with cowboys and drovers and a few prospectors.

"It's that," Ella said without a smile. "It's interesting and it's a one-man show, and that man is Caleb Burr. Speaking of which, he's coming our way."

Gabe looked ahead to see a man driving a fine carriage with two matched sorrels that would have caught the eye of horse fanciers no matter what part of the country.

Caleb Burr really did resemble a boar hog. The rich man was huge, round-shouldered, triple-chinned, and he must have weighed at least three hundred pounds. He was dressed in a black suit with a massive gold chain draped across his ponderous belly. He had little, deep-set black eyes and a pug nose. His balloon cheeks were red and whiskerless.

"Ain't he a sight, though," Ella whispered, "and guess who he intends to bed and whose ranch he figures to buy?"

Gabe had no trouble guessing, especially when Burr pulled in his matched sorrels right in the middle of the street so that no one could go around him and then said to Ella, "My, my, I always thought mourning was something that should not last very long, but you appear to have set the record, Ella. Yet, poor taste and men's clothes can't hide the fact that you're still the handsomest woman in southern Colorado."

Ella's cheeks flamed. "I haven't the luxury of mourning," she said in a hard voice. "I've got a ranch to run."

Burr grinned and glanced at the horseman who flanked his carriage before he winked and returned his attention to Ella. "I think I have a solution to your problems. Sell out to me."

"No thanks."

"It's me—or no one." Burr was leering at Ella.

His confidence raised Gabe's hackles.

"You'll sell," Burr said, "one way or the other, Ella, you'll sell. And the price will go *down*, not up."

The man was threatening, and that rankled Gabe plenty. He looked aside at Ella and said, "Do you have any more to say to this . . . this man?"

"No," she said, her voice thin with fury, "please drive on to general store."

Gabe slapped the lines against the dapple's rump but before the mare could move out, the horseman grabbed its bit.

"Let go," Gabe ordered.

The gunman replied, "I don't believe Mr. Burr said he was through talking with Ella, mister. I don't believe you was given permission to take your leave."

Gabe studied the gunman with an intense dislike. He was a man whose sole purpose in life was to intimidate, or kill on order. Gabe knew his type well and understood that such men took strength from the weakness they found in others.

"I think you'd better let loose the mare's bit," Gabe said in a soft voice.

The horseman's lips cut a thin smile. "Is that right? Well maybe I ought to teach you to think before you open your big mouth."

The gunman released the bit and started to reach for his gun, but he froze when he saw Gabe's Colt suddenly appear with its barrel trained on the spot between his eyes.

"Now," Gabe said, "will you and your fat boss man just get the hell out of our way before I decide to get rough?"

"Why you son of a bitch!" the gunman snarled. "Next time—"

Gabe didn't wait to hear what the man intended to do the "next time" they locked horns. He raised the barrel of his pistol just a fraction of an inch and squeezed the trigger, blowing the gunman's hat clean off his head.

"Next time," he said, "I'll put the bullet between your eyes."

The gunman went pale.

"Who the hell is this man Ella?" Burr demanded.

"Just a friend," she said, suddenly looking as radiant as if the sun were shining again.

Burr's beady eyes never left Gabe's face. "Mister," he grated, "I better not *ever* see you in this valley again or your hide is going to be tacked on my barn door. You understand me?"

Gabe nodded. "I think you've made it pretty clear. But I'll let you in on a little secret—I'd planned on leaving this valley today, but you've just given me a reason to change my mind. I'll be seeing you around, Caleb."

Gabe gave the mare a smack on the rump with the lines, and the dapple headed on down the street. Ella grabbed his right arm and squealed with joy. "You were wonderful!"

"I sure don't like that man," Gabe said.

Ella's smile faded. "I'm afraid that, if you stay, Mace really will try to kill you. And even if you kill him first, there will be others."

"It's a free country, ain't it?" Gabe said. "It's free to go or stay where you want and where you're wanted."

"And I definitely I want *you*, Gabe."

"Then I'll stay awhile until Mr. Burr and his heavy-handed friends come to understand that a man don't like to be run off or threatened."

Ella nodded. She touched Gabe's cheek and patted his arm. "You can have everything I promised last night . . . and more, if you want."

He turned to look into her face and, as he had expected, she was blushing like a schoolgirl. "I think I'm going to want plenty," he said, "but I'll choose when. Okay?"

She nodded and sniffled with happiness before she said, "Pull up over there in front of that store. We'll get everything we need for the winter now, before Caleb thinks to order the owner not to sell to me."

Gabe did not intend to stay for the winter, but he'd stay for however long it took.

CHAPTER FOUR

Big Caleb Burr was steaming by the time he reached his headquarters and stomped into the two-story log house that boasted more square feet than most territorial governor's mansions.

Mace Frazier followed his boss inside, and when Burr's current mistress, a big-breasted prostitute who went by the name of Lulu, came weaving into the room with a full glass of whiskey in her fist, Mace tried to wave her to silence.

But Lulu was too drunk to take a hint. Dressed only in a red silk nightgown that showed more of her than not, she placed one hand on her curved hip and demanded, "Well, Caleb, what the hell is the matter now?"

"Shut up and get out of here so we can talk!" the rancher bellowed.

Lulu lifted her chin, made a ridiculous effort to pivot around with some dignity, lost her balance and almost fell before recovering to stagger out of the room.

"I thought I was going to be rid of her in a couple of days!" Caleb swore. "And that she'd be replaced by Ella Porter. Now, I got to keep that drunken bitch in whiskey until I get Ella and her ranch in my grasp."

Mace refrained from comment. He'd learned quickly that the best way to handle Caleb Burr when the big rancher was incensed was just to keep his mouth shut and nod his head until Caleb ran out of steam.

"I *want* the Porter widow!" Caleb shouted. "I've wanted her from the moment I first set eyes on her five damn years ago and neither of us are getting any younger!"

Caleb swung around toward the door. "You hear that Lulu?" he bellowed. "Your ass is gone when I get Ella into my bed! Gone! So drink while you can, you sot, because your days are numbered!"

They both heard a muted curse in the hallway and shattering glass. Nobody needed to tell Mace that Lulu was throwing a fit. This house was a lunatic's den and, if the job had not paid so damn well, Mace would have ridden out a long, long time ago and gone back to his old occupation of being a bounty hunter.

"Damn!" Caleb swore. "Who the hell was that stranger?"

"I don't know, but I mean to find out in a hurry," Mace vowed.

"Find out? You'd better either run him off or kill the bastard, get rid of him one damn way or the other!"

"Yes, sir. But I thought you wanted me to take care of Chet Dodson first. He's supposedly coming into town for supplies tomorrow. I got things arranged so he'll have little choice but to fight."

Caleb went to his liquor cabinet and poured three fingers of imported French brandy. He tossed it down and felt heartburn but poured another anyway. The second one went down a whole lot smoother, and Caleb visibly relaxed. There was simply too damn much at stake to lose control, and the doctor said his heart was not strong enough to take a lot of unnecessary excitement. Getting all worked up and having a heart seizure was something he had to be careful to avoid at all costs.

"All right," Caleb said, forcibly lowering his voice, "you're correct in reminding me about Dodson. He was the only rancher with any backbone besides old Ed Porter. Once Dodson is out of the way, the others will quickly sell their spreads, and I'll finally have control of this whole damn valley."

"Do you want me to tell you how I'm going to goad Dodson into drawing his gun?"

"No," Caleb snapped. "Tell me the details when you've finished the job. After Dodson is taken care of, I want you to take care of whoever that big son of a bitch is that was driving Ella's wagon. You understand me?"

Mace nodded. "It'll be a pleasure, though he showed he's damned fast."

"So what?" Caleb challenged. "I'm paying you top dollar because you're supposed to be faster than whoever I send you up against. If you're slowing down, Mace, say so and draw your wages so I can find a younger man."

Mace's cheeks flamed with anger and humiliation. "I'm only thirty-three, Caleb. I'm as fast as I ever was with a gun and a damn sight more clever. The man I am today would have killed the man I was five years ago."

"Aw bullshit," Caleb growled. "You're slowing down because you've passed your prime. As for being smarter, well, I'll give you credit for that much. But that stranger was smart enough to get the draw on you right in the middle of my town, and it made the both of us look like a pair of fools."

"Yeah," Mace said, for he had been thinking the same thing, "but at least now there will be no surprises."

"There damn sure better not be," Caleb warned, "because I'm not paying you three hundred dollars a month to get shot out of the saddle or buffaloed like you was today."

Again, Mace felt his cheeks burn with embarrassment. Caleb Burr would not soon let him forget how some pumped-up bastard had gotten the drop on him.

"I'll take care of the big man with the buffalo coat," Mace promised, "right after I eliminate Chet Dodson."

"See that you do," Caleb said, as he slammed his empty glass down and left the room.

Mace waited until he heard the boss man's door bang shut and then he went and poured himself a full water glass of Caleb's imported brandy. He took the brandy over to a horsehair sofa in front of the dwindling fire of the fireplace.

"Conchita!"

A short, dumpy Mexican woman with gray hair and missing teeth scurried into the room. "Sí señor?"

"Put some damned wood on the fire and fix me some supper, then bring it out here."

"Sí Señor Mace!"

Conchita hurried out of the room, and Mace smiled to hear the servant woman yelling orders at the other workers as the kitchen went into action. A few minutes later, a Mexican lad of about ten rushed into the room with an armful of wood. He was in such a hurry and his arms were so overloaded that he dropped a piece, tried to pick it up, and spilled the whole bundle.

Mace glared his disapproval, and the boy shrank from his hard eyes. "Pick it up, Manuel!"

"Sí señor!" the boy whispered in fear as he scrambled to snatch up the wood and feed the fire.

"Now get out of here and tell them to hurry up in the kitchen," Mace growled when the fire was coming to life again.

The boy started to turn and run across the floor, but Mace

grabbed his arm and said, "Bring me that decanter of brandy over there on the table."

"Decanter, señor?" The boy did not know the word.

"That fancy bottle, you stupid little greaser!"

The boy darted over to the table.

"And if you drop it," Mace hissed, "I'll cut your ears off and roast them over the fire, then make you eat them."

The boy's good command of English was demonstrated by the way his face paled. He held the decanter with both hands as he hurried to Mace's side and gave it to him, his chin trembling with fear.

"Now get out of here," Mace spat. Manuel did not need to be told twice.

Mace ate on the couch, sipping more brandy than he'd intended and eating his dinner. He knew that Caleb had probably also taken too much to drink and then fallen into bed early. The man was the early to bed and early to rise type. He awoke in the morning before daylight, had a huge breakfast in the kitchen, and then retired to his bedroom to pour over his ledgers and account books, probably needing to remind himself every day how wealthy he was becoming.

"Hey," Lulu whispered as she came padding across the room late that evening when Mace was starting to doze off and the servants had long since gone to bed.

Mace's eyes popped open when Lulu sank down on the couch beside him and then began to unbuckle his belt and loosen his pants.

"Now just what the hell do you think you're doing out here in the main room?"

Stung by Caleb's cruel words, Lulu had sobered up some and even taken a bath. She smelled of enough cheap perfume to kill flies at fifty paces, but her eyes were bright with mischief and she was smiling lewdly.

"I think you can guess what I'm up to," she whispered.

Mace knew he should stop her before this went any further. If someone happened to walk through the room and see them fooling around, word about it might get back to Caleb and there'd be hell to pay, even though the rancher didn't give a damn about Lulu.

"This is crazy," Mace said as he wound his fingers through Lulu's long, brown hair, "but I don't believe I'm going to stop you."

"I didn't think you would," Lulu whispered in a throaty voice, her lips glistening in the firelight.

They made love on the couch, and when they were done, Mace said, "If Caleb ever caught us doing this . . . why, he'd hire enough gunmen to blow me to little pieces."

"He'll figure it out sooner or later," Lulu said. "So why don't we get rid of him before he gets rid of us?"

"Are you serious?"

"Of course." Lulu poured them both more brandy, emptying the bottle in the process. "He'll get rid of us before long. Both of us. He thinks you're too damn old and I'm not worth keeping because I drink too much and he wants that Porter woman. So why wait until we're tossed out without so much as a thank you for our services? Why not kill *him* and then *we'll* be the ones running Mesa and los Osos Valley? We can do it, Mace!"

Mace stood up, and stared at the fire as he sipped the brandy.

"I just don't know," he said quietly. "I'm not the only gunman on his payroll. If anything went wrong, then we'd be as good as dead."

"The stakes are high both ways," Lulu said. "We got everything to lose . . . but also everything to gain. I'm a gambler, aren't you?"

Mace turned to look into Lulu's eyes and he thought that, if she had been a man, she'd have been his enemy. But since she was a woman, maybe they could make a winning pair.

"Let me think on it some," he said. "I've got to take care of Dodson tomorrow, and there's some meddlesome stranger that's staying with Ella Porter. I need to handle him, too, before I can think about what you said."

"Why wait?" Lulu started to reach for him again, but Mace took a back step.

"Now just slow down, Lulu. You're movin' a little fast." Mace finished his brandy. "I'll put some thought to what you said. Killing Mr. Burr would be the easy part, surviving whatever he will have put in store for us would be another thing altogether."

Lulu's smile slipped. "What do you mean?"

"I mean the man prepares for *everything*," Mace explained. "He'll have thought about being betrayed, and he'll have someone or something in the wings to even the score, even after his death. I just feel in my bones he would. A man like Caleb Burr would haunt you from his grave."

Lulu's face suddenly twisted in fury. "I hate him!" she swore. "He's cruel and mean. He makes us grovel under his thumb. Even you, Mace. I've seen and heard how he's treated you like you were a slave. He's cussed you up one side and down the other and you just stood there and took it."

"Shut up!"

Lulu realized she'd pushed things too far. "I'm sorry," she said, "but it's just the way Caleb is, and I say we shouldn't have to put up with it anymore."

"I'll think about it," Mace said, putting down his glass and turning to go to bed.

Lulu grabbed his hand. "Don't you want any more lovin'?"

Mace was tempted but shook his head. "I got to get some sleep. I'm killin' a man tomorrow, and I need to be sharp."

"I wish you were killin' Caleb instead of Chet Dodson. It's Caleb that is our enemy, not that poor rancher."

"Caleb is paying my way, not Dodson," Mace said. "It's just that simple. The fact that I like one better than the other don't mean spit."

"What will happen to the other ranchers?"

"They'll have a meeting and raise a big fuss. Caleb will listen and maybe even some territorial marshal will put me under arrest for a little while. But what it all comes down to is that there won't be a trial. I'll be let go, and the ranchers that last the winter will be plenty ready to sell out come next spring."

"And since grizzly hibernate, there won't be any more attacks." Despite the heat of the fireplace, Lulu shivered. She'd had nightmares about the killer grizzly. She could not think of a more horrible way to die than in the jaws of a savage creature.

"Yeah," Mace said, "the bears will hibernate until next spring. But there are wolves aplenty in los Osos Valley and they'll be runnin' wild during the wintertime. Just like they always have."

Lulu looked up into Mace's eyes. "You're the only wolf I want runnin' wild on me, big boy."

He chuckled as he headed for his bedroom and sleep. "Lulu," he said over his shoulder, "you are a real charmer."

She watched him go and then sank down on the horsehair couch and studied the flames, wondering if Mace was man enough to dare kill Caleb and let her take the rancher's place as head of a growing mountain empire of logging, mining, and cattle.

Lulu had sneaked into Caleb's bedroom where he kept his financial records and she'd studied them long enough to know that there was a fortune to be made by a woman smart enough to grasp the opportunity.

And she would, even if Mace would not.

CHAPTER FIVE

On the way back from their shopping trip in Mesa, Ella Porter had fallen into a thoughtful silence that lasted until they neared the boundaries of her ranch.

"That stream over there marks the northern edge of my ranch," she said, pointing to a pretty creek that meandered through the meadow toward the large and swift los Osos River.

She twisted around on the seat of the buckboard and pointed again. "The eastern boundaries go right up into the forest for about a mile and then turn south to the end of the valley."

"It's a fine spread," Gabe said. "Be worth a lot of money if you can hang onto it."

"I think so, too," she said. "Like I told you, the timber rights alone are going to be worth plenty some day."

"Why don't you see if you can find some logging company?"

"No chance," Ella said. "Everyone knows that Caleb Burr runs this valley."

"It won't always be that way," Gabe said.

"It will as long as Caleb owns the only sawmill in Mesa. No Gabe, I'm afraid there's no other market for timber in these parts. He's the only one that will buy cattle, too."

"It's wrong for one man to have that much power," Gabe said, "but it's not uncommon."

"Maybe not," Ella said, "but Caleb is the one that's ruining everything. And if he can't buy or freeze you out, he uses the threat of Mace or some other gunmen to make people knuckle under."

"I've seen it many times before," Gabe told her. "Often as not, a man starts out with all the decency in the world and all the best intentions. But once his business prospers, he turns greedy and wants to have the whole pie for himself. Money and power corrupt."

"Yes," Ella said in agreement. "I understand that when Caleb first come to this valley, he was a good man. He hired a ranching foreman named Heck Thompson who did everything right and then, when Heck asked for a percentage of the profit, he suddenly disappeared and was never seen or heard from again. My guess is that Caleb had him murdered."

"Most likely," Gabe said, "but you'll never know. How many hard cases does Caleb have on his payroll?"

"You mean gunmen?"

Gabe nodded.

"Besides Mace, maybe two or three—but they're not always around. I think he just keeps Mace as protection and hires the others as he needs them. The trouble is, most everyone in Mesa owes him money. He either owns their land or his bank has a mortgage on their business."

"It's hard to stand up to a man who can take your home or business away whenever he wants," Gabe said.

"And also their jobs. You see, Caleb's sawmill employs at least twenty workers, most of them with families. His mining operation isn't as big, but he's the one that doles out the payroll."

"So what you're saying," Gabe commented, needing to know what he was really up against, "is that Caleb Burr controls most everything in and around Mesa."

"He's the judge, jury, and the executioner, too," Ella said.

Gabe found that hard to swallow. "Isn't there a town constable or sheriff?"

"Nope. Like I said, Caleb is the law."

"No he isn't," Gabe argued, "because Colorado is a United States territory. The folks over in Denver are pushing hard for statehood, but until they get it, what you are living in remains a territory run by federal law. That means that there is a territorial marshal in charge of keeping order in Mesa. Wherever he is, that man is the one that has the authority to curb Caleb Burr's abuse of power."

"Sure," Ella said, "the marshal's name is Dwight Flowers. He rides through once in awhile and when he comes to Mesa, he stays at Caleb's ranch house, eats at his table, and drinks his imported liquor. Marshal Flowers also purchases his supplies in Mesa at a discount because of Caleb and gets his drinks free in our saloons. Does that tell you how much good the marshal is for people like me?"

"I'm afraid it does," Gabe said in a tight voice.

"So what are we to do?"

Gabe thought on it a moment and said, "If the law doesn't work, you have to change it. Where's the marshal's office?"

"Over in Cripple Creek. You ever been there?"

"Can't say as I have," Gabe admitted, "but I may have to pay the man a visit if he don't come around soon."

"And what good would that do seeing as how Marshal Flowers has both his hands in Caleb Burr's pockets?"

Gabe rubbed his chin. "I don't know for sure," he confessed, "but it seems to me that most men are smart enough to figure that they can't take money with them to an early grave."

Ella's eyes widened a little, but she said nothing as they continued on to her cabin.

She fixed supper that evening while Gabe cleaned his weapons and then pulled out his mother's worn, dog-eared old Bible.

"I didn't know that the Sioux believed in Jesus Christ," Ella said.

"They don't. But my mother did. You see, she was in about the same boat that I am now. She'd been raised white, but found much to her liking about the Oglala. My stepfather, Little Wound, was as fine a man as you'd ever want to meet. He raised me just as if I were his own flesh and blood. I never wanted for anything, and I was treated by every member of the tribe just as if I was a full-blooded Oglala."

"But your mother kept her Bible." Ella came around behind Gabe and stared down at the opened pages which were filled with little comments and prayers. "Your mother wrote all that in such a small hand?"

"Yes," Gabe said. "She didn't have anything else to write on, and she figured that a Bible would be treated so that her words would last."

Gabe's big hand rubbed the worn leather binding. "It's from this Good Book that I know and remember my mother best. You see, Ella, she also taught me to read from this Bible because she knew that the way of the Oglala was passing. She understood that I had to be able to live in the white man's world or I would be killed."

"Your mother sounds as if she was a very wise and loving woman."

"She was," Gabe said, gazing down at the Bible and letting it bring back the memories of what had been a happy childhood until the white soldiers had come and the Plains Indians' world of free roaming and buffalo hunting had forever changed.

Ella sensed that it would not do to ask this man any more questions so she washed the dishes and read a book of her own until she grew sleepy. But every few minutes, she would glance over at Long Rider and imagine how it would feel to be married to such a man.

Ella felt guilty thinking about what it would be like to feel his muscular body against her own, to taste his mouth and make his heart pound with desire. Such thoughts made Ella's cheeks burn, but she could not keep her mind from them. Edgar was barely planted, and it was not right to think of another man so soon, but still, she wondered how it would be to make love to Gabe Conrad and thought it would be better than anything she had ever known.

Under cover of her blankets, Ella considered throwing caution to the wind and getting up to lie beside this man on the floor, but she knew instinctively that he would be repelled by such brazen behavior so she blew out her reading candle and tried to go to sleep.

The next day, Gabe set about working on the ranch yard despite the stiffness in his shoulder. He mended fences and greased the hubs of a broken down wagon, intending to fix its axle when his shoulder felt stronger. He found that Edgar, while not an orderly man, had prized good tools and owned both an anvil and forge. The man had been something of a craftsman and had built things to last, especially the house, barn, and corrals.

That night, his shoulder pained him a good deal, and Ella was faintly scolding when she said, "You can't work that hard yet. Tomorrow, I want you to take it easy."

"All right, then what can I do?"

Ella knew what she wanted to do with this man, but she

looked away so that he could not read her desire and said, "Let's go for ride and count my cattle."

"All right," Gabe said, "we'll need to know if we have enough hay to winter them and that would be a good, easy day for us."

Early the next morning, Gabe saddled both the buckskin and the dapple mare. Not long after sunrise, they rode the perimeter of her range, most of which bordered heavy pine forest.

"Edgar told me he thought we had less than two hundred head left," Ella said as they took their count. "But I know we lost a hell of a lot last winter to the wolves and even more last summer to the grizzly."

"You sure of that?"

"What do you mean?"

"I mean that maybe you're losing more to cattle rustlers than to wild animals."

"Not very damn likely," Ella said, her face growing stiff with anger. "Look over there."

Gabe followed her eye to the edge of the valley where three cows had been trapped in deadfall against a rotting log and torn apart by what could only have been grizzly.

Trotting over to the slaughtered stock, Gabe dismounted and handed his reins to Ella, then inspected the cattle and the tracks that surrounded the bloody ground.

"They were killed about a week ago," he said, "and since then, they've been fed upon by wolves, coyotes, and smaller animals.

"But they were killed by grizzly, weren't they?"

"Yeah," Gabe told her. He sorted out the tracks until he found one clear imprint of a bear's paw that had not been trampled by the scavengers. He stared at the grizzly bear's track with more than a little interest. "Well, I'll be!" he exclaimed.

"What's wrong?"

"Nothing is wrong, just different."

Ella dismounted and led their horses closer. The horses, eyes rolling with fear because the carcasses of the cattle were ripe and the scent of the grizzly still strong, pulled back, but Gabe grabbed the reins and yanked them forward.

"Look at this bear track," he said, pointing to the ground.

Ella studied it and said, "I've seen too damn many like it already to be interested."

"I find it *very* interesting," Gabe said. "How can you fail to notice how the bear is missing all but two toes on his right front paw?"

"I guess you're right," Ella said, shrugging her shoulders to show that this revelation did not seem all that important to her. What mattered were the three dead cattle.

"If this is same grizzly that has been raiding your herds, then we can track him a whole lot easier."

"I thought I explained that there are dozens of grizzly that have been raiding. This valley is a haven for grizzly."

"Maybe so and maybe not. I'm sure there were hundreds around here once, but it's been my experience that grizzly learn to shy away from mankind. Most of the grizzly are either killed off by men, or they go deeper into the wilderness where they can't be reached. Ella, there's a chance that you're dealing with a rogue bear that's been crippled, shot, or in some way lamed up and is too slow or old to catch deer or bring down elk."

"I'd like to believe that," she said, "but I just can't. I remember Edgar telling me how he came upon a clearing and saw dozens of grizzly bear tracks. As I recall, it was about this time of year, just a month or two before the grizzly go into hibernation."

Gabe found that difficult to believe. "They're not herding

animals, Ella. And while they might fight over a fresh kill, they don't run in packs."

Ella climbed back on her horse. "The only thing I know is that Edgar saw a lot of grizzly tracks."

"Did he mention if any of them were missing all but two toes on the right forefoot?"

"No."

Gabe mounted his nervous buckskin. "Let's count your cattle," he said, reining away.

With a final backward glance at her poor cattle, Ella said, "At least I won't have to worry about feeding those three this winter."

"Things are going to change for the better," Gabe promised.

Ella struggled to believe him. "They have to," she said. "I lost my husband and now these cattle. My herd is down to practically nothing. We used to have fifteen or twenty good saddle horses, but the grizzly either killed them or ran them off."

"If there were more daylight and the tracks hadn't been washed away by that last storm, I'd see what I could do to track that two-toed bear," Gabe said. "A good bear dog wouldn't hurt, either."

"There aren't any left in this valley," Ella said. "The grizzly either killed them or ran them off, too."

Gabe wasn't listening as he rode away. He was thinking about the two-toed bear and wondering about all the grizzly attacks in this valley. Something was just not right about this whole thing. Grizzly *didn't* run in packs.

Gabe wanted to track this bear in the worst way, but that could take days, perhaps even weeks, and he could not afford to leave Ella alone. He'd seen the lust in Caleb Burr's eyes for the young widow and the hatred that had burned in Mace.

Gabe was pretty sure that he would either be forced to kill Mace and Caleb Burr or be killed himself. A two-toed killer grizzly sure wasn't the biggest threat facing him in this damned valley.

CHAPTER SIX

When Caleb Burr arrived at his office located in Mesa's only bank, one of his clerks hurried outside to take charge of the pair of matched horses.

"Morning, Mr. Burr," the clerk said with forced cheerfulness. Quickly he added, "Morning to you, too, Mace."

Mace didn't bother to reply because he was preoccupied with the thought of killing Chet Dodson. The man had not been in town for supplies all week, but today Caleb had sent for him and that meant Dodson would be arriving in Mesa this morning.

When the clerk led the horses and carriage off toward a stable where they'd be kept until Caleb was ready to go home, the cattleman said, "Mace, when Dodson arrives, I'm going to give him one last chance to sell his ranch before I have you gun him down."

"He won't sell."

"Maybe not, but it would be easier for me to buy him out than to wait until the court puts his place up for public auction or, even worse, some shirttail relative arrives to claim his land holdings."

Mace didn't care. Actually, he sort of liked Chet Dodson so that killing the rancher would bring him no pleasure.

"So how am I going to know if Dodson decides to sell or not?"

"If I shake his hand as he leaves the bank, then it will mean he's finally agreed to sell. But if we *don't* shake, then I want you to see that he doesn't reach home."

"Whatever you say."

Mace needed a drink to quiet his stomach and steady his hand before Dodson arrived. He started to ride away, but Caleb's voice, low and filled with anger, brought him up short. "And there's something else we need to talk about."

Mace swallowed. He could tell by Caleb's hard expression that he wasn't going to like what the man had to say. "And that is?"

"I'm bringing in a new man to back you up."

"I don't need any damn help! What the hell you want to bring in someone else for?"

"Because I won't tolerate hired hands drinking my best liquor and humping my women!" Caleb hissed.

Mace paled. His mouth opened but then clamped shut because he realized that a denial would only make things worse. Caleb knew about him and Lulu and, to Mace, this was as good as hearing his own death sentence.

"You hear what I'm saying, Mace?"

"Yes sir," he replied. "But I . . ."

"Shut up! Just take care of Dodson if he's still too stupid to sell out to me today."

Mace nodded and rode away, knowing that not only was he going to be replaced by a younger, faster gun, he might wind up disappearing just like old Heck Thompson had disappeared several years ago.

As Mace headed down the street, his mind churned with panic and desperation. He was trapped, and his only chance was to either just ride straight the hell out of Mesa and never look back or else join forces with Lulu and kill Caleb before his own death warrant was signed, sealed, and delivered.

"Howdy, Mace," a logger said as Mace dismounted and tied his horse to a hitch rail before the Mesa Saloon. "Say, do you feel all right?"

"Sure! Why wouldn't I?" Mace snarled.

The logger shrank from the gunfighter's sudden anger. "No reason. You just look a little pale this morning. I was just being friendly is all."

"You better get yourself a pair of damned spectacles," Mace snapped as he finished tying his horse up and went into the general store to buy some of his own whiskey and a couple of cigars before he settled in to wait on Chet Dodson's arrival in town.

When Dodson rode into Mesa, he was astride a mule named Sarah that he claimed was smarter than a good many people. Sarah was a big, long-legged mule, and she could run faster than most horses. Her only fault was that when she got to running, she'd bray so loud you could hear her coming or going for about a mile, and her huge ears would rotate like ceiling fans.

"Howdy, Chet!" several people called as he and Sarah moved down the street to the bank. "How's Sarah today?"

"Well," Dodson said, "as you can plainly see, she's feelin' and lookin' right perky."

Dodson's infectious smile and cheerful manner had a way of making other folks smile. Even his appearance and manner were a little comical. The rancher was awkward looking, slender with a protruding Adam's apple. He stood six-foot-five and had a habit of tripping over his own feet when he was distracted, which he seemed to be most of the time. He was a confirmed bachelor, very shy and uncomfortable around women but a favorite among men.

Dodson always wore the same sorry brown hat that drooped down toward his shoulders and the same old patched leather jacket with the wool lining all rubbed off the collar. He had little wire-rimmed glasses and sometimes rode into town sucking wetly on an empty corncob pipe. He drank in the saloons, but only milk or sarsaparilla, and he was the butt of many good-natured jokes.

Dodson looked and played the fool, but those who knew or watched him carefully came to realize in a hurry that Dodson was neither. The truth of the matter was that he was deceptively strong and, if the jokes on him got mean or ugly, Dodson was plenty willing and capable of using his bony fists to bloody a leering face.

Even his eyes were sharper than they first appeared. Dodson's spectacles were almost clear glass and served him best when he was looking at far away things, like sunsets and mountaintops. But up closer, certainly within pistol range, his eyes were keen enough to put a bullet in a man-sized target. Dodson was not a gunman, but the pistol on his lean hip was not for show. He was quick and accurate. Mostly though, Dodson was a good cattleman who only feared one thing—the killer grizzly bears that had long plagued his herds.

"Mornin', Dodson," Caleb Burr said, stepping up to the door of his bank with an outstretched hand. "Good of you to come in since I heard you been feeling poorly the last few days."

"I feel a whole lot better now," Dodson said, reluctantly shaking Caleb's sausage-fingered hand without enthusiasm. "What did you want to talk to me about, Mr. Burr?"

"Come on inside and sit down," Caleb said with a broad smile. "I don't think we need to do business out in the street."

"I don't think we need to do business at all," Dodson said around his corncob pipe stem.

"Well, we'll see. Could be I got something to say that might just change your mind."

"I doubt it," Dodson said, following the rich man into the bank. When they were seated, Caleb ordered hot coffee and while they waited, he tried to get the man to talk. "Terrible thing about Edgar Porter getting killed by grizzly," he said, knowing how much Dodson feared the beasts, "just terrible."

"It sure was," Dodson said, not wanting to think, much less talk about it.

"Weren't you mauled pretty bad years ago by a grizzly?" Caleb asked, knowing the man had been attacked and bore scars on his arms and chest.

"I was," Dodson said. "So what did you ask me in to talk about?"

Caleb smiled. "I still want to buy your ranch. How much did I offer you last spring?"

"Five thousand, but I wouldn't sell it for—"

"I'll give you six," Caleb said, cutting the man off. "Six thousand in cash. For that kind of money, you could buy a bigger and better ranch down in the New Mexico Territory where they don't lose their cattle and horses to grizzlies. Where a man can sleep at night without having a rifle at his side just waiting to hear those beasts coming after his poor stock."

"Six thousand is a lot of money, but it's still not for sale. You know the timber alone is going to be worth that much some day."

Caleb's smile tightened, and he leaned forward across his desk. "What the hell good is it if you get caught someday out on your range by that killer grizzly?"

Dodson paled a little. "Well, I just won't! That's all! I keep out in the open and carry a buffalo rifle under one stirrup and a Winchester carbine under the other. Ain't no grizzly going to attack a man out in the open."

Caleb leaned back in his chair. "I suspect that Ed Porter died because he shared that same illusion. But we both know that, even though his body was found just inside the forest, he would have been riding his boundaries when the grizzly came charging out of the trees. When it did, Ed's horse probably whirled and dumped him and . . . well, I'm afraid it's obvious what happened after that."

Dodson swallowed noisily. He put his pipe in his coat pocket and rubbed his hands together, discovering they were clammy with sweat. "I got things to buy, then I'd best get back to the ranch."

"I'm glad you think so," Caleb said. "Now, if you could just make the grizzly in these parts believe that, then you'd really have something."

Dodson pushed his long frame out of the chair. He had not even tasted his coffee. This conversation had soured his stomach. "Be seein' you," he said as he started to leave.

But Caleb grabbed his sleeve. "Seven thousand cash. That's your last chance to sell out and start over with a bundle of cash. I know how you feel about the grizzly. Hell, a man shouldn't have to wake up nights in a cold sweat remembering how he was almost eaten alive by one of those creatures."

Dodson yanked his arm free. "I just don't want to sell!" he protested in anger. "I just want to be left alone to raise cattle. I got a real strong feeling for this valley."

Caleb sighed. "Well," he said, "I understand."

"You do?"

"Sure. I just hate to think that you might wind up the same as Edgar Porter did. It must have been a terrible way to die. The man was fortunate the grizzly snapped his neck quick."

"Stop it!" Dodson was on his feet heading out the door. Caleb followed him and when he caught Mace's eye, he nodded and then turned around and went back inside to drink his morning coffee.

Mace had waited patiently until Dodson had stuffed his purchases into a canvas sack tied behind his cantle. When the man rode out of town, Mace slipped into an alley and mounted his horse. About four miles south of Mesa, the road crossed a shallow stream. That's where Mace figured he would meet Dodson and goad the cattle rancher into a gunfight.

It was a pity Dodson had not accepted Caleb's offer to sell his ranch and pocketed thousands of dollars in cash. Had that been the fortunate situation, Mace would have killed Dodson, then robbed him and left this accursed los Osos Valley a happy and wealthy man.

CHAPTER SEVEN

Early that morning, Gabe examined his left shoulder in the firelight while Ella changed his bandage as she had every morning and evening since he'd arrived at her ranch cabin. "It looks to be healing clean," he said.

She glanced up to meet his eyes. "Yes, but I'm afraid that there will be some prominent scars."

"I don't care about that," Gabe said, rolling the shoulder back and forth and finding no stiffness at all. "I've got a pretty good collection of scars already."

Ella nodded. "They're all over your chest, some on your back, arms, hands. Gabe, I've never seen a man as scarred as you. What were you raised by, a den of panthers?"

He managed a faint smile. "I've seen a lot of action in my lifetime. When I was a boy raised by the Oglala, we were taught how to ignore pain. Battle scars on a warrior were considered to be badges of courage."

Ella traced one pencil-thin scar across Gabe's broad chest. "What caused this one?"

"A soldier's saber," Gabe said, moving his finger over to a round white scar at this side. "And this one was from a bullet I caught down in Texas. I was ambushed outside of San Antonio and left for dead."

"You've had a hard life, haven't you?" Ella said. "And a dangerous one."

Gabe frowned, and the firelight gave his skin a luster like polished copper. His torso was scarred, but it was also beautifully muscled. He was broad across the shoulders and narrow in the waist, and although he lacked the thick, bulky muscles of a laborer, there was no questioning the fact that he could combine power and speed.

Ella brushed her fingers lightly across his chest, swallowed, and said, "My late husband was . . . well, he wasn't put together anything like you."

Gabe looked down to see desire on Ella's face and as her fingertips brushed back and forth across his chest, he could feel his own hunger grow. He took Ella's fingers and kissed them and then drew her into his arms.

"I just want you to understand that I'm not the marrying kind, Ella. I don't want your heart to be broken."

"It won't be," she whispered, stepping back from him and unbuttoning her woolen shirt.

"Don't you think we'd better get over to that bed of yours?" he asked.

She nodded, smiling.

For a long, long time after they made love, they lay in each other's arms, breathing together.

"Are you all right?" he asked finally.

"Yes," she told him honestly, "but after that, I'll never be the same woman I was before. Now that I know what it's supposed to be like, I won't ever be satisfied with less."

"I might have created an insatiable monster," Gabe said.

"I think you have," she replied. "And from now on, we're going to do less work outside and more of this inside."

Gabe smiled.

"I'd like to spend the day here," he said, "but I need to get my horse shod in Mesa today."

Ella sat up quickly. "I wish you wouldn't go to town," she said. "I'm afraid that you might run into Mace and something terrible could happen."

"If it's going to happen, putting it off won't help. My shoulder is healed enough that I can handle Mace with either my gun or my fists. I won't hide in your bed, Ella."

She kissed his mouth and said, "I wish we could stay right here in bed until spring. I don't think I could ever get enough of you. Not by half, I couldn't."

With an amused chuckle, Gabe rolled out of bed and dressed. It was already two hours past sunrise, and there was much to be done. Besides getting his horse shod, they needed some supplies.

"Can I ride along with you into town?"

"I'd rather I went by myself," he told her as he strapped his six-gun on his hip. "If there's trouble, then . . . ."

"Then I need to be there," she said, jumping out of bed and grabbing her own pants and shirt. "I couldn't be easy a minute while you were gone. I *have* to come. Maybe, if I'm at your side, Mace or some other gunmen on Caleb's payroll won't try and challenge you."

Gabe didn't believe that for a minute, but he saw that arguing would be futile so he nodded and headed for the door. "I'll be in the barn getting our horses ready."

"I'll be right along," she promised.

They rode out fifteen minutes later and put their horses to a ground-eating gallop that devoured the miles. It was nearly eleven o'clock when they spotted a rider about a mile up ahead.

"Recognize him?" Gabe called.

Ella stared intently but shook her head. "Not yet."

Gabe slowed his buckskin to an easy trot and Ella matched his pace. Gabe couldn't be sure, but he had a hunch that the man far up the road was Mace. And then suddenly, another rider appeared from the direction of town.

"Why that's Chet Dodson!" Ella cried with alarm. "I can tell because he's the only one in these parts that rides a mule!"

"I think the first one is Mace," Gabe said. "Any idea why he'd be waiting on Dodson?"

Ella cried out with alarm and then began to whip her horse into a run. "He must mean to kill him!"

Gabe reached for his six-gun, thinking that a shot would distract Mace from his intent or at least flaw his concentration. But before he could get his Colt out of his holster, Gabe saw both men go for their weapons. One shot was fired and Dodson slumped on his mule which bolted into a braying run. Mace lifted his gun and fired at Dodson's back. He missed and gave chase.

Gabe's own pistol bucked in his fist and although the man was far out of his range, the shot caused Mace to pull his horse to an abrupt halt. He took one glance at Gabe, then reined away and spurred hard for Mesa.

Gabe let the gunman escape, knowing that he could easily find him at Caleb's ranch headquarters or in town. The main thing to do right now was to overtake that runaway mule and try to save Dodson's life.

CHAPTER EIGHT

Gabe passed Ella on her mare and spurred hard after the mule. He had never seen a mule that was as fast or as noisy as the one that Dodson was riding. It took him nearly a mile to overtake the damn thing, grab its reins, and pull it to a halt. The moment that he did, Chet Dodson keeled over and toppled to the ground.

Gabe bailed out of the saddle and when he rolled Dodson over, he could see that the man was in a bad shape. Mace's bullet would have penetrated Dodson's heart if it hadn't been deflected by a silver dollar stuffed in his shirt pocket. As it was, the bullet had ricocheted off the dollar and entered Dodson's chest just under the collarbone. The only saving grace was that the wounded man was not coughing or spitting up bright red blood which would indicate that he had been lung-shot.

When Ella reached the scene, she took one look at Dodson and said, "We've got to get him to Doc Landrum's place!"

"I thought you said there wasn't any doctor in Mesa."

"I did. The Doc lives in an high-mountain cabin about eight miles west of here. He's a loner who hates people."

"So what makes you think he'll help this man?"

"Dodson once saved the doctor's life," Ella said, pulling a handkerchief out of her pocket and pressing it to the hole in Dodson's upper chest.

Gabe stood up to leave. "I'll have to take your mare back to the ranch and get the buckboard. This man is in no shape to ride even one mile, let alone eight."

"You couldn't get a buckboard over the trail to Doc Landrum's place."

Gabe frowned. "If the man can't ride, walk, or use a wagon, I guess that leaves us with damn few choices."

"You could make a travois, couldn't you?" Ella asked.

"Yeah," Gabe said. "I guess that would work. But it'll be a rough ride."

"Not any rougher than a buckboard would be over a rocky mountain trail."

Gabe had to agree. Without further discussion, he caught up his horse and Dodson's mule, then galloped them back toward Ella's place. Using an ax, it took him less than thirty minutes to convert a pair of lodgepole pines and a piece of canvas into a travois. Due to years of practice, he was able to quickly lash the poles down on either side of Dodson's mule.

"Make yourself useful, you lop-eared cuss," he growled at the mule as he remounted and headed back to pick up Dodson. Sarah went along, but she didn't like the travois dragging behind her and went braying at every stride.

By the time he returned to Dodson, Gabe was about ready to shoot the damned fool mule. But he was cheered up considerably to see that the wounded man was at least conscious.

"Let's get him loaded up and tied down or he'll bounce off," Gabe said as he eased the man onto the travois.

The movement caused Dodson to rouse in pain, and he said, "I can ride Sarah."

"Oh no you can't," Ella told the wounded man as she helped tie him down. "We're going to the Doc's cabin, and you know how rough that trail is."

Dodson nodded. "It'd be smoother going down river rapids, Missus Porter."

"I know," she told him, "but the Doc is the only one that can save you now, Chet. You've just got to hang on and hope Doc isn't off somewhere's."

Dodson's face was very pale. His breathing was shallow, and it was clear that he was in real pain.

"Here," Ella said, removing the man's wire-rimmed spectacles, "these might bounce off so I'll keep them safe for you."

"Thanks," Dodson said. "I sure don't mean to add to the troubles you've already got, ma'am. I just . . . ."

Ella placed a forefinger over his lips. "I'm not the one that needs the worrying about right now," she said.

Ella climbed on her mare and took Sarah's reins. "Let's go!"

Gabe yanked his rifle from its scabbard and followed behind as they jogged across the valley and plunged into the forest. The instant they were in heavy forest, all of Gabe's instincts sharpened in the expectation of a bear attack. As a rule, grizzly would stay clear of men, but the los Osos Valley grizzly were a highly aggressive breed and therefore the exception. They'd smell Chet Dodson's blood and the horses, and they just might come looking for an easy meal.

The trail that Ella followed was faint and either washed-out or overgrown with manzanita and other dense shrubbery in many places. At best, there were times when Gabe couldn't rightly see any trail at all. They would ride straight up to a log or some deadfall, and he'd swear that Ella was lost and that they'd have to ease the travois back around and retrace their steps. But about the time he'd be craning his neck and planning their retreat, Ella would fool him and a path would open.

Dodson was in a hell of a lot of pain, that much was obvious. While Gabe had gone back to the ranch to make the travois, Ella had unsaddled her horse and cut her own saddle blanket into strips which she'd used to bind Dodson's wound tight so that the man didn't lose any more blood than necessary. Even so, the tall, slender rancher was as pale as sandstone and after a few miles of being bounced up and down over the rocks, he'd mercifully lost consciousness.

In the heavy forest a man couldn't see more than thirty feet in any direction. Gabe was plenty busy keeping his eyes open for grizzly, but felt fortunate to see nothing more threatening than deer grazing in an occasional meadow, lots of birds, and plenty of squirrels.

"How much farther?" Gabe called up to the woman after they'd ridden nearly two tedious hours.

"Another mile or two," she said as they crossed a swift mountain stream then angled around a scree of moss-coated rocks. They attacked a shale-covered mountainside and followed a narrow trail that had more turns than the tracks of a desert sidewinder. Higher and higher they climbed and if Dodson had not been lashed down tight and the mule so surefooted, Gabe was certain they'd have lost the man and his travois in a terrible wreck that would have ended up down in a brush-choked canyon.

Had it not been for Dodson and the travois, Gabe would have enjoyed the scenery. There were magnificent vistas that a man could watch for hours. He saw golden eagles nesting on a rocky pinnacle and, here and there, wispy waterfalls that would turn into raging torrents come springtime.

But Gabe didn't have the luxury of sight-seeing on this

trip. He kept a sharp eye on Dodson and never relaxed his vigil against a possible grizzly attack. Once, he threw his rifle to his shoulder and almost unleashed a shot but held off at the last moment when he realized that he was about to open fire on a fat brown bear with a cub at her side. The bear caught their scent from a quarter mile away. She stood up on her hindquarter, nose sniffing the wind, poor eyes doing her little good. She woofed a few times, then dropped down on all fours and went lumbering off into the forest, the cub in her wake.

It was mid-afternoon when they finally topped a low, rocky ridge and gazed down on a beautiful alpine lake with about a mile of heavily forested shoreline.

Gabe wasn't sure what he had expected, maybe a little mining settlement or something, but not this kind of pristine isolation. "A doctor lives clear up here by himself?"

"I told you he doesn't like people."

"Well, I hope he likes grizzly because he must see his share of them," Gabe said, noting a set of wicked claw marks high up on the side of a big pine tree.

Ella hurried her mare down the steep, rocky slope. The mule kept pulling back on its reins, placing each foot down as if it expected to drop through a hole in the earth.

Mules were like that. You could force a horse to move faster than was safe over a bad trail, but not a mule. Gabe knew well that if they were crowded too hard, they'd just dig in their hooves and refuse to move, and then you'd be stuck until the damn things decided that you had been taught a lasting lesson.

"I just pray that the Doc is still here," Ella said. "I haven't seen him since early spring, and anything can happen to an old man alone up in country like this."

Gabe agreed. It was wild and beautiful up here, but the living would be a daily struggle. Exposed up near a high ridge like this, the blizzards would be ferocious. And if a man alone broke a leg or got himself in a fix, well, he'd be a goner before he could get help.

"There's his cabin," Ella said, pointing to a little inlet on the lake about a mile away.

Now Gabe saw the cabin. It was low but pretty good-sized and right near the water, situated out on a little peninsula. "I see smoke floating up from that rock chimney."

"Thank God!" Ella exclaimed when they reached the shoreline and headed toward the cabin.

When they were still a hundred yards from the cabin, Gabe saw a little puff of white smoke erupt. An instant later, he threw his rifle against his shoulder and aimed at the cabin. "He's firing on us!"

Ella tore off her old hat and waved it around overhead. "Doc!" she cried. "It's Ella Porter and Chet Dodson! Don't shoot!"

One more bullet whistled overhead and then there was silence.

"He heard me," Ella said, pushing her horse on down the trail.

"No wonder he don't get along with people given the way he greets them," Gabe said, resting the Winchester across his lap and riding on.

Doc Landrum came stomping out of his cabin, a bandy-legged man that reminded Gabe of a cranky little elf. He was short of stature with a long white beard and a potbelly. His nose was red and his eyebrows were white and bushy. He wore a coonskin cap and a redcheckered shirt, the kind favored by many logging men. Only the big-bored rifle in his chubby little fists looked intimidating.

"Ella, what the hell are you doin' bringin' half of Mesa up here with you?" the little man snapped.

"I'm sorry, Doc. Chet was shot a few hours ago, and I

didn't think he'd make it without your help."

"Who the hell is the big jasper?" Doc growled, raising the barrel of his rifle threateningly at Gabe.

"He's my . . . my friend," Ella said simply. "He's helping me fight off Caleb Burr and he's twice had a run-in with Mace and beat him."

"That the truth?" Landrum challenged.

"She's embellishing it a little," Gabe said, "but I don't like to see people get pushed off their land when they don't want to leave. So I sort of figured I'd take a stand down in that valley and see what it brought me."

"You must be even dumber than you look," Doc Landrum growled. "What it'll bring you is a damned bullet! That's what you'll get."

Gabe could not help but bristle a little. "I'm not the easiest man to kill," he said. "A lot have tried, but now some are dead themselves."

"Humph!" Landrum grumped, sizing Gabe up and then turning to the travois.

The doctor jerked a big hunting knife from its sheath and bent down over Chet Dodson. He took the man's pulse and then appeared to almost gouge his eyeball out when he thumbed up his eyelid and studied his eye.

"How long has he been unconscious?"

"About an hour," Gabe said. "It's a hard trail up here."

"I know that!" The doctor cut the bandaging away and examined the bullet hole. It was a surprisingly clean entry hole. From a distance, it appeared like a large mole. Just a round, dark spot under the clavicle.

The doctor slipped his forearm behind Chet's neck and eased him into a sitting position, then ripped his shirt away to study the man's back.

He dropped Chet back down and his brow furrowed with concentration. "Missed the lung, huh?"

"I believe so," Gabe said.

"Well, so do I," the doctor replied, " 'cause if it hadn't, the man would already be long gone from this world. We need to get him inside and then dig out that bullet."

The doctor sheathed his knife and scowled. "Mister, you look strong enough to beat bears with a willow switch. Grab him under the arms and I'll take his legs."

"No," Ella said, stepping in between them. "Gabe's shoulder is just healing up and if he tries to lift that much weight, his wounds might tear open."

Gabe wanted to protest but before he could do so, Landrum himself was cussing and grabbing Dodson under the shoulders. Gabe and Ella each took ahold of one of Dodson's legs and they carried him into the cabin.

The cabin was nicer by far than Gabe had expected. Like Ella's place, it had a real wood floor and a good stove. But the most astonishing thing was that the doctor had constructed and beautifully carved a floor-to-ceiling bookshelf that covered one entire wall and was filled with books.

"Don't just stand there gawkin'!" Landrum bellowed. "Go get some wood and help Ella fire the stove so I can have some boilin' water."

Gabe didn't like to be ordered around by anyone, but he figured that this was not the time or the place to make it an issue. Besides, it was obvious that Landrum was just a mean-spirited old hermit who didn't like anyone, including himself. Gabe had met dozens of prospectors, hunters, and similar types of men who were afflicted with the same miserable dispositions. Landrum had done the right thing by coming up into these lonely forests and staying far away from the rest of mankind.

When the water was boiling and Ella had plenty of rags, Landrum cleared off a heavy log table for Dodson.

"Tie the man down, all fours to the table's legs," the

doctor said, tossing Gabe and Ella strips of rawhide. "And then, mister, I want you to sit on his gut and try to keep him in one place when I start digging for the bullet."

Gabe nodded and when he was positioned on Dodson's stomach, he said, "He won't move on you."

"The hell he won't."

Landrum selected a pair of long, shiny forceps from a worn old medical kit. "This is going to be rough. Might even kill him. But unless we get that bullet out, he's a goner anyway."

The irritable doctor pulled his hunting knife from his sheath again. He wrapped a strip of wet cloth around the handle and his fist, then went over to his stove, opened it, and shoved the blade into the flames.

The doctor held the knife into the fire until the cloth that covered his hand began to steam and then he retracted his hand and knife. Gabe could smell burning hair and the blade was smoking.

"I guess that will do it," the doctor said as he returned to Dodson's side. "Ready?"

Gabe nodded and pressed down hard on Dodson's shoulders. "Let's get this done with."

"I agree," the doctor said as he plunged his blade into Dodson's bullet wound and then used its sharp cutting edge to saw a hole big enough to work inside.

Dodson awoke with a terrible scream and damn near bucked Gabe to the floor. The man was slender, but amazingly strong. If his limbs had not been tied to the table's legs, he would have thrown Gabe across the room.

"Ride him down," Landrum ordered. "Ride him down flat!"

"I'm doing my best," Gabe gritted as he pressed down hard and the doctor jammed his forceps deep into the bubbling wound.

Again, Dodson bucked and screamed, but then his body went limp.

"Is he dead?" Ella cried.

"Nope," the doctor said, his face bent over close to the wound as his hand worked the forceps. "He ain't dead, but he probably wishes he was."

Ella turned away, but Gabe watched intently because he'd had to dig a few bullet holes out of people and it never hurt to watch someone else's technique, especially when they were a hell of a lot more experienced.

The doctor, for all his poor manners and terrible personality, was good. Gabe didn't miss the way he concentrated on the forceps, his eyelids drooping as he used his sense of touch more than his sight. He seemed to hold his breath and go still except for his right hand. In less than a minute, his lips pulled back from his teeth in a grin.

"Got it!" he cried, yanking the forceps and the slug out in triumph. "Is he still breathing?"

"Barely," Ella said.

The doctor studied the smashed lead slug. "Yes sir, Colt .44. If these were made of gold instead of lead, I'd be a rich man by now."

Landrum dropped the slug and forceps onto Dodson's chest, then said to Gabe, "You can climb down now because this man won't move anymore until he regains consciousness."

"Will he be all right?" Ella asked.

"Yes," Landrum said. "But if you'd have waited a day or I'd been off prospecting for that gold your husband once found, our tall friend would have been a goner."

Gabe climbed back to his feet and rubbed the blood off his hand onto his pants. "You are a very skillful man, Dr. Landrum. It's too bad you aren't in some town where you'd be saving more lives."

"I'm saving my *own* life by being up here, young man. That's the life that has to be most important. It took me thirty years to realize I couldn't help others unless I first helped myself."

Gabe nodded, feeling a little foolish because the doctor was right. Gabe did not know or care why Landrum had taken a dim view of mankind and had gotten himself into such a bad state. Quite often, frontier doctors wound up raving alcoholics. They were sensitive and caring men who found themselves helpless to save most of their patients so they used drink to numb their disappointments.

The doctor opened a vial of powder and sprinkled it onto the wound. "This seems to help make wounds heal clean," he said. "I get it from an old Ute medicine man. When it comes to native medicines, I don't care who makes them as long as they work. And this stuff does. I used this powder only last week to heal up the stump of a racoon whose leg I had to amputate. The amputation healed as clean as anything."

The doctor rebandaged Dodson's wound and then cleaned his forceps and knife before he walked out of the cabin and headed down by the lake, head bent forward, hands clasped behind his back.

"Where's he going?"

"For a walk," Ella said. "The Doc, he can't stand to be around people too much anymore. He just needs to be alone a lot. He's come to like animals better than people."

"Can't say as I blame him in some cases," Gabe said as he studied the doctor thoughtfully and decided that he was a good man, despite his odd ways and many shortcomings.

CHAPTER NINE

Caleb Burr steepled his pudgy fingers together and glared at Mace with barely concealed fury.

"So you don't know if you killed Dodson or not, is that what you're saying?"

"I might have," the gunman said too fast. "I put a bullet into his chest, I can swear to that."

"Then you should have put one more before you ran!" Caleb swore, pounding his desk. "You didn't finish the job."

"There's no way that Dodson can survive that bullet," Mace said. "No way at all."

But Caleb sneered. "You make me sick! All I've been hearing from you since Ella's friend showed on the scene is a bunch of excuses. Nothing but excuses! And now, even if you did kill Chet Dodson, there are two witnesses. So where does that leave us?"

Mace licked his lips nervously. "They saw it happen, but they were too damn far away to see who drew their gun first. I can claim that I fired in self-defense, and no one can prove me wrong."

Caleb muttered and pushed himself to his feet. "It should have been easy," he said. "All you had to do was kill Dodson and do it without anyone seeing you. The man was popular. There will be a big stink over this and since you are on my payroll, guess where that puts me in the picture. I don't like it, Mace. I don't like the way you've handled this at all."

"Well, I'm not too damn happy about how things worked out either," Mace said. "So maybe I ought to kill them?"

Caleb shook his head. "Not Ella. Kill her meddling friend and do it right away."

Anxious to leave, Mace stood up. "Mr. Burr, you said something about hiring another gunfighter to help me. I been thinking. Maybe I could use some help when I face Ella's new friend."

"No," Caleb snapped. "You've made the mess we're in, now get out of it by yourself!"

Stung with humiliation, Mace turned on his heel and left the rancher's study in a hurry. He was moving across the porch when Lulu stepped into the corner of his vision.

"Mace?"

"Not now! Stay away from me!"

But Lulu wasn't the kind of woman who would be easily denied and she said, "You better talk to me or you'll have no one to watch your back."

Mace stopped in his tracks because the whore was right. Lulu, for all her drunken brassiness, was in his corner and would help him if she thought he had a chance of killing Caleb and coming out on top of this game.

"All right," Mace said in a low voice. "Meet me after dark in our usual place."

"Why wait?" Lulu asked. "Caleb knows all about us anyway."

"That's true enough," Mace said as he pushed on, "but I think we'd be crazy to rub his nose in our dirt."

Lulu's eyebrow arched up, but she smiled before she went back inside to pour herself a much-needed drink.

She went straight to Caleb's liquor cabinet and that's when her eyes opened wide because the cabinet was locked! It had always had a little lock built into the door, but Lulu had never even realized that Caleb would have the key, much yet use the lock.

She tugged firmly on the cabinet door at first, then harder and harder until the bottles inside rattled. In desperation, she looked around the room, hoping that Caleb might have left a bottle or two out. But he hadn't, and she had not even thought to sneak a few into her room.

Damn!

"What's the matter?" Caleb said from the hallway.

Lulu spun around to face him. He was leering at her and that made her angry. "You know what the matter is. Open this thing up!"

"No," Caleb said, advancing a few steps. "Not for you, I won't."

Lulu swallowed noisily. "Well then I'm out of here," she announced. "I'll just pack my things and leave right now!"

He laughed in her face and said, "It's a long, long walk into Mesa and even if you got there without being eaten by a grizzly or raped and killed by someone, it wouldn't help your problem."

"Why not? I *need* a drink, Caleb. That's all I want."

"No," he said, his voice hardening.

She stomped her foot down. "Then I'll get one in town and the hell with you! We're finished!"

Lulu started to leave the room, but Caleb stepped into her path and something in his eyes told her to stay back where he couldn't reach her. For all his fat, he was incredibly strong. His thick fingers and bloated hands had the power to effortlessly crush her windpipe.

"Please," she whispered, "just let me go away. You can

have any woman you want, Mr. Burr. *Any* woman. You don't need someone like me."

"You're right for once," he said. "But I want to watch you suffer a little before I let you go. You've humiliated me and now it's my turn. That's why, even if you escape this ranch, it would do you no good. You see, I've let it be known that, if anyone sells or offers you a drink in my town, they're going to be sorry."

"You can't do this to me!"

Caleb smiled. "Oh no? Then why don't you walk your pretty ass into Mesa and find out?"

Lulu nervously licked her lips. "Listen," she stammered, "I know that you don't give a damn about me for anything but your bed, but . . . ."

"You got that right," Caleb said, "and for the last few weeks, I haven't even had that questionable pleasure."

Lulu took a deep breath and forced a smile. She knew how to handle a man—any man. All she had to do was use her body to bend his mind to her own advantage. "Maybe I have been a little . . . I don't know . . . Preoccupied."

"You've been drunk and screwing Mace every chance you get. That's what you were going to do now. Get drunk on my liquor and meet him tonight. Isn't that right?"

"No!"

Lulu moved across the room, hips swaying provocatively. When she reached Caleb's side, she slipped her hands around his fat neck and ground her pelvis against him. "Honey, I know I drink too much sometimes, but I'll behave from now on."

"Will you?"

Lulu nodded eagerly. "Yeah. Starting right now, if you want."

She rubbed her breasts against his chest and planted a wet, disgusting kiss on his porcine lips. "I just forgot for

a while who takes care of me, Caleb. You're the man that
I'm here for, not Mace."

He smiled into her pretty but frightened face. "You're
scared half to death of me, aren't you, Lulu?"

"Scared?" Lulu giggled, but it sounded bad. "Now why
should I be scared?"

"Because I'm going to make you pay, baby," he swore,
tearing her hands from around his neck and dragging her
down the hallway toward his room.

"No, please!" she sobbed.

A Mexican house servant appeared for an instant and
Lulu screamed, "Help me!"

The woman's hands flew to her face. She made the sign
of the cross and vanished down the hallway.

Lulu screamed again, but Caleb picked her up and threw
her across his shoulder as he carried her down the hallway
toward his room.

"I'm going to see if a whore like you can be taught the
meaning of loyalty," he swore, kicking open his door and
throwing her at his bed. "And by the time this lesson is over,
you'll be begging for a chance to prove yourself to me!"

Caleb began to tear off his shirt. "You hear me, Lulu?
You'll be begging!"

Late that evening, Mace waited nervously for Lulu inside
the main ranch barn. Everything inside of him said to just
saddle his horse and run for his life, but Lulu had planted
an idea inside that could not be shaken and which held him
almost as if against his own will. Over and over a voice kept
repeating in his head that, if he and Lulu could eliminate
Caleb, then everything on this ranch and the better part of
Mesa itself would be theirs. They could build an empire
and . . . .

"Mace?" The voice belonged to a woman, but it didn't

sound like it belonged to Lulu. It was high and frightened.

"Over here," Mace called as he struck a match and lit a candle.

Lulu slipped out of the shadows and when Mace saw her battered face, he took an involuntary step backward. "My God! What happened?"

Lulu couldn't stop shaking. "He figured it was pay-back time for me," she whispered. "And he pays back real good."

Mace knew that he should take the poor woman into his arms and comfort her but with Lulu's eyes almost swollen shut and her lips all smashed and caked with blood, he didn't want any part of her.

"Lulu, I think—"

"I want you to kill him for me. Kill him *right now*, Mace. Just go into the house and shoot that fat son of a bitch to death!"

He swallowed. "I'd never get off this ranch alive. You know that. We can kill him, but we got to do it so it looks like someone else pulled the trigger."

She didn't seem to be listening. Her shoulders dipped and she bent her head down and sobbed into her hands. When she finally looked up, she said, "Then you won't do it for me?"

For some reason, the way she said that caused a shiver to travel up and down Mace's spine. "Well, sure I will, but we got to plan it out and . . . hey, what are you doing?"

Lulu was advancing and when she was ten feet from him, she reached into her dress and pulled out a derringer. She cocked it and pointed it at his chest. There was no way that she could miss.

"Now wait a minute!" Mace whispered, wondering if he could distract her for the instant it would take him to draw his gun and put a bullet through her chest. "Honey, I—"

"Reach across your body with your left hand and lift your gun out of your holster," she ordered in a still, dead voice.

"Lulu, I swear I'll kill him! But we need to plan things a little and—"

"One more word and I'll pull the trigger, Mace. I swear I will!" she cried, her voice almost breaking with hysteria. "Now take your gun out and drop it on the ground! Slow and easy."

"All right. All right! Just don't do anything crazy on me. We need to talk. Better yet, you need a doctor. We can ride south and find one. I know where we can find one by tomorrow morning."

"Your gun!"

When his gun was out and on the floor, she said, "Now move back a few steps."

He obeyed her, his eyes never leaving the barrel of her derringer. It was an over-and-under, two shot model, .45 caliber. It was plenty capable of stopping him dead in his tracks.

"This is crazy! Lulu, you were always right. I should have listened to you days ago when you said that the only way we could get what we wanted was to work together."

"Too late now."

"But it's—"

"Kneel on the floor, Mace, and put your wrists together behind your back."

"What the hell are you going to do to me?" he screamed.

"Just do it!"

Mace did as he was told. He dropped to his knees and put his hands behind his back and realized he was bathed in a cold sweat.

"Now what?" he asked as she moved behind him and used a cord to tie his wrists behind his back.

"Lulu, please," he begged, "I love you! We can have all of this! I'll go inside the house and kill him right now if you want!"

"It's just too damn late," she sniffled as she finished tying his wrists together, then stepped around in front of him and pointed her derringer at a place between his eyes.

"No!" he cried, knowing he was about to die.

Lulu started to pull the trigger.

"Wait!" a voice said from the doorway. "I have other plans for him."

She glanced over to see Caleb enter the barn. His voice was almost gentle now as he said, "Lulu, you can go back inside now. You did just fine."

"A drink," she whispered desperately. "I *need* a drink."

"I left a bottle of my cheapest whiskey on the cabinet top," Caleb said. "You look like you finally have a real excuse for drinking it."

Hope made her smile with gratitude, but smiling caused her lips to split and she whimpered.

"Get out of here," Caleb said.

"Wait a minute!" Mace cried. "Lulu, if you leave me with him, I'm a dead man!"

"You're a dead man either way," Caleb said. "We're going to take a little ride in my carriage. You've never ridden in it before, have you, Mace? Not unless you've been having Lulu on my fancy felt seat cushions, which I wouldn't put past you. Well, no matter, because tonight it is my turn to have some fun."

Mace's mind reeled with the possibilities that faced him before his death. He was sure that he would die in screaming agony. Caleb was a twisted monster and after seeing what he'd done to Lulu, Mace knew the man was going to torture him worse than any Apache might have done.

"At least I always killed men clean!" Mace cried, as he

summoned his reserves and climbed to his feet. "I faced men and shot them down clean. I never tortured them!"

Caleb walked swiftly over to him and his boot came sweeping up, driving between Mace's legs so hard it lifted him off the ground and dropped him back to the earth, writhing and screaming.

A few minutes later, the huge rancher threw Mace into his carriage and drove off into the night, whipping the sorrels into a hard gallop.

As the carriage swept out of the ranch yard tilting on two wheels, Lulu staggered outside with a bottle of whiskey upraised in her fist and cried, "Goddamn it, Mace, I loved you! And if you'd have had the backbone, we could have had all of this!"

But her words were beaten away by the sound of the team's drumming hoofbeats.

CHAPTER TEN

Gabe finished cleaning his six-gun and his Winchester rifle. Outside the doctor's cabin a cold wind was blowing and there was the hint of another storm coming in from the north. Gabe had been on this high mountaintop for three days, and he was restless to be on his way.

"I'm going back to the valley today," he told no one in particular.

The doctor looked relieved, but Ella was quick to protest. "But it would be better if you stayed here until Chet is strong enough to also come down."

"No it wouldn't," Gabe said. "Chet's in no shape to ride yet, and you've got that purebred bull in the stone corral that's gonna be half starved by now."

Ella had forgotten about the bull. She had, however, pitched it a great pile of hay before they'd left, but a large animal like that would consume a great deal, especially in this cold weather.

"Perhaps you're right," she said.

Gabe looked over at Chet. "I can also stop by your ranch and check up on things."

"I'd be grateful," Chet said. "It's just me and an old man named Luther Rote that's taking care of things. Luther probably figures I either got myself killed or I got bought out and ran off and left him to face our troubles alone."

"I doubt he thinks that," Gabe said, "but I'm sure he's mighty worried by now. And there's no telling what kind of trouble Mace and Caleb Burr are brewing."

Chet nodded. "You tell Luther that if they come gunnin' for him, he's to just leave and not fight. I won't have his death on my conscience."

"I'll tell him," Gabe promised as he checked the action on his gun and then slipped it into his holster.

Doc Landrum cleared his throat, an already familiar habit he used before speaking. The doctor didn't say much, but when he did talk, he got right to the point. "You gonna go after Mace?"

"I'd rather see if I can roust out the United States marshal to arrest him for shooting Chet."

Doc snorted. "Don't you understand that the man is in Caleb's back pocket?"

"So I've heard," Gabe replied. "But at least I can start out doing things the right way. And if the marshal won't do his job, then I'll already have tried to use the law and have some excuse for taking things into my own hands."

"It will be your own hands alone," the doctor said. "Nobody left in the valley will stand against Caleb Burr and Mace."

"Why don't you wait until this bullet hole of mine heals a little more?" Chet said. "I already know that I'm not as fast on the draw as Mace. Never expected to be. But I can shoot what I aim for, and I wouldn't run out on you in a tight spot."

"I know that," Gabe said. "I can't make the mistake of riding into Caleb's trap and getting out alive. I'll just let it be known that I'm expecting the U. S. marshal to do his job and, if he doesn't, I'll do it for him."

"I hope you realize that's the kind of talk that will bring Mace to you in a big hurry," Chet said.

"That's my hope."

Gabe pushed himself up from the table. While he was eager to leave, he was also a little sorry because it was beautiful up in this high mountain country and he'd gotten to know Chet and the doctor well enough to believe they were both fine men.

Each had problems, Doc with not being too friendly with other men and poor Chet because he was so bashful around women. But Chet might soon discover himself enjoying women. Ella might be the best thing that could have happened to the shy rancher, and who could tell, perhaps love might even blossom between the pair. They both had the same interests and a love for the valley below. It would be a good match, a far better match for Ella than he'd ever have been.

Gabe shook hands good-bye with the two men and went outside with Ella. He looked up at the sky again and said, "If I push that buckskin of mine right along, I'll get off this mountain before the storm hits."

"You be real careful," Ella said. "If Mace gets it in his mind that you're too dangerous to face, then he'll look to ambush you with a rifle."

"That's what I'm expecting," Gabe said. "And don't worry, this white Oglala has eyes in the back of his head. I'll stay out in the middle of the valley where I can't be pot-shot and I'll keep my guard up every minute."

Ella kissed him on the lips. "I'm sorry we haven't had time to . . . well, you know."

Gabe was amused. "You mean get together real close like?"

She slipped her hand around his waist. "You know that's exactly what I mean. But we'll have the whole winter to do nothing but make love and feed my livestock."

"We'll see," Gabe said. "The main thing is, I feel good about you and Chet being up here. Doc is pretty savvy to the woods. I don't think anyone is going to get the drop on him."

"We'll be fine," Ella said. "I doubt if Caleb and his men even know about this hideaway cabin."

"Maybe and maybe not," Gabe said. "Just keep that mule of Chet's out in front. She's the smartest and the noisiest critter I ever saw. If anyone comes near, she'll be the first to spot them and start hee-hawing."

"Yes," Ella promised. "We'll do that."

Gabe saddled his horse, tied his gear behind his cantle, and headed down the mountain at a good, fast clip.

The storm broke on him sooner than he'd expected. When he was still a couple of miles from Ella's cabin, huge hailstones began pelting downward, smashing against the trees overhead and shattering ice all over Gabe and his buckskin.

Gabe pulled his hat down tight and rode on, listening to the thunder roll and hearing the sharp crack of lightning. The lightning was striking the highest peaks, and across dark, rolling clouds, Gabe could see it sparking off the tops of the tallest trees. Once, a huge bolt of lightning shivered downward not more than two hundred yards away and struck a big pine whose top exploded in a shower of sparks. The sharp smell of smoking wood filled Gabe's nostrils and the gelding between his legs became half wild with fear.

"Easy," Gabe said, patting the animal's neck and keeping it moving forward. "We're going to get off this mountain yet."

The sleet turned to snow about the time that Gabe finally reached the valley. The wind and rain were making the meadow grass thrash like a wheat field standing in the face of a tornado. Gabe put his buckskin into a hard run and by the time he arrived back at Ella's cabin, he was wet and shivering.

The first thing Gabe did was gallop toward the stone corral, intending to feed Ella's poor bull. But the moment Gabe saw the corral, he blinked with shock. The gate to the stone corral was made of thick saplings about as big around as a man's calf. They were piled one on top of the other seven feet high. But now, they'd been half torn away, and the buckskin between Gabe's legs was snorting and rolling its eyes in fear.

Yanking his Winchester from its scabbard, Gabe hopped off his horse, the hair on the back of his neck standing on end as he moved cautiously toward the broken gate. He wasn't at all sure what he'd find inside the stone corral, but he was pretty damn certain that it wouldn't be a live bull.

The day was fading fast and with the dark clouds overhead, the light was poor at best. Gabe levered a shell into his rifle. He was just now recovering from one wrestling match with a grizzly and the very last thing he wanted was more of the same.

Gabe took a deep breath and jumped into the gateway, half-expecting to come face to face with a grizzly feeding on its kill. Instead, he saw the bull lying half devoured on its side and beside it, also ripped open and torn apart by a grizzly, he saw what was left of Mace.

Gabe lowered his rifle and turned away for a moment. He'd been prepared to find a dead bull, but not a man. And not *this* man. Turning back, he moved inside the corral, then dropped to one knee and studied the tracks that were already starting to be washed away.

"The two-toed bear," he whispered to himself. "No doubt about it."

Gabe went over to kneel beside the remains of Mace. It was a terrible sight. Something no child or woman should ever have to witness and one that a man would not soon forget. The grizzly had nearly torn Mace's head off and his throat was . . . well, it wasn't very pretty.

Gabe stood up, wondering why Mace would be inside this corral. Unless the man had decided this would be the best place for his ambush. That reasoning made sense. Gabe reached down and extracted the man's six-gun. Mace had been an expert with his Colt and should have been able to mortally wound a grizzly with six bullets even if they were too light to stop the wounded grizzly from taking his life.

The gun had not been fired! It was fully loaded.

Gabe shook his head. "Something is wrong here. If Mace came up and the grizzly was already inside the corral feeding on Ella's bull, then he would have heard it and had a chance to either get on his horse and get away or at least reach the safety of the cabin. And at the absolute least, to have gotten off a few rounds before it killed him."

Gabe moved around the inside of the corral, seeking any kind of clue as to what might have happened in this little arena of death. The snow was falling heavily and, in a few more minutes, there would be no hope of discovering any information so he had to do what he could as fast as possible.

But there was nothing to see in the corral that told him anything other than that the bull, the bear, and the man had all been inside the corral, and only the grizzly had walked away when the dust had settled.

Shaking his head with confusion and shivering from the cold, Gabe went back outside, leaving Mace right where he'd been found. The snow was already covering both carcasses and they would freeze solid if they hadn't already.

Gabe fixed the corral gate as best he could and walked his horse over to the front of Ella's cabin. "Horse," he said, "I guess you're going to be my fresh bait tonight because I'm tying you right to the front door. And if that grizzly comes back to feed, he'll smell you and come running. But don't you worry, I'll get him before he gets us—I hope."

The horse stamped its hooves nervously on the cold ground. Gabe unsaddled it and got the horse a stack of Ella's winter hay before he went into the cabin and stoked up the fire.

It was going to be a long, stormy night. Just the kind of night that a grizzly used to hunt if it didn't first take a notion to search out a cave somewhere and start thinking about hibernation.

Gabe hoped that it was still too early for bears to hibernate, even in this high country. One thing for sure, he wanted that two-toed bear before it hibernated because otherwise the creature would prey on his mind all winter.

Gabe sank down in a chair before the fire and rubbed his hands together briskly in an attempt to warm them. He stared into the flames and tried to organize all his jumbled thoughts and impressions so that they made sense.

The big question—the one that made no sense at all to his way of thinking—was why hadn't Mace at least gotten off a few rounds before the bear killed him? Had the man been drunk? Or perhaps the grizzly had caught him off guard or even asleep in his blankets.

Naw, Gabe thought, rejecting that idea. "There hadn't been any blankets and there wasn't even any sign of hoofprints," Gabe mused aloud.

Gabe frowned and said, "But then, if the man had been waiting in ambush, he would have left his own horse hidden in the forest somewhere out of sight. Pity that poor animal," Gabe said, imagining that the horse would have suffered the same fate as Ella's purebred bull.

Gabe heard his horse stamping nervously. He snatched up his Winchester and jumped outside, heart hammering against his ribs, half-expecting to see a grizzly right in his face.

Only there wasn't any grizzly. There was only the storm and his poor, miserable horse. He could certainly have put it up in the barn, but that wouldn't give him any warning if the grizzly returned. Hell, the bear could feed half the night and then disappear in the snow and Gabe wouldn't have any way of knowing.

"I'm afraid you're the freshest bait on the ranch tonight," he said. "Sorry, but sometimes life works that way."

The buckskin nickered and nuzzled him as if pleading and it was all Gabe could do to shut the door on the creature.

CHAPTER ELEVEN

The next morning when Gabe awoke, he quickly pulled on his boots and clothes, then stepped out the door into a foot of fresh snow.

His gelding nickered softly and Gabe untied the horse, then walked it around the yard, ending up at the barn. He saw no sign that a grizzly had been anywhere close to the ranch.

"Here," he said, opening the barn door and turning the gelding loose inside where it could eat all it wanted. "I guess you deserve a reward."

The gelding went straight for the hay. Gabe closed the barn door and latched it securely before he trudged back to the cabin and stoked a fire. Then Gabe brewed himself a cup of coffee and fried some beef and potatoes for breakfast. As he ate on his feet, Gabe stared out at a blanket of glistening snow. The snow wasn't deep, only about a foot, and the sun was coming up strong so that it would melt by mid-morning.

When Gabe finished his breakfast, he went outside and found a shovel to bury Mace. But then he changed his mind and took an old blanket from Ella's bed and went back to the stone corral.

Standing over Mace's frozen body, he said, "My hunch is that Burr ordered you to come here and ambush me. And since you worked for him, I think it's only fitting that *he* should be the one to bury you."

The mutilated corpse stared up at him with wide, frightened eyes. Gabe wrapped it up and then had to decide how he would transport it to Caleb's ranch.

It seemed to Gabe that he only had two choices and they were either to hitch up Ella's creaky old buckboard or to fashion a new travois. After some deliberation, Gabe decided that it was time to find out whether or not his buckskin was broke to pull in a wagon.

The buckskin wasn't near ready to quit eating and it was cantankerous when Gabe struggled to put it in a harness.

"Dammit," he said, "everybody in life has to do things they don't enjoy. That includes the both of us. If you think I'm looking forward to pilin' that frozen corpse into the back of a wagon and then delivering it to a den of snakes, well, you got another thing coming. So hold still."

The gelding had little choice but to obey Long Rider. It allowed itself to be hitched to the buckboard but when Gabe climbed up into the driver's seat, the fool horse bolted and ran.

"Whoa!" Gabe shouted as the wagon shot across the yard, weaving and tipping dangerously in the snow. "Dammit, whoa up!"

Fortunately, the fool buckskin came right up against the forest and had little choice but to stop. Fuming with anger, Gabe strong-armed the gelding and got the buckboard turned around and headed back toward the stone corral. The buckskin was snorting and dancing, but Gabe knew that the horse would settle into its role after a few miles of dragging the buckboard through the soft blanket of new snow.

It wasn't very pleasant loading Mace's frozen body into the wagon bed. When he was finished, Gabe went back to the cabin for his Winchester. He had no idea what to expect when he faced off against Burr and his crowd of cutthroats. But one thing was sure, they weren't going to be welcoming him with hot chocolate and cookies.

The buckskin was so fractious that Gabe lost patience, pointed it north up the valley, and let the damn thing have its head and run. The moment that the buckskin discovered that there was no longer any pressure on the lines, it took off like a scalded cat. After a mile or so of tugging the buckboard through the snow, however, its lungs were working like a blacksmith's bellows, and although it was still cold, the horse was drenched with sweat.

Gabe pulled the animal to a stumbling walk, and when they came to a shallow, ice-crusted stream that meandered down to los Osos River, he allowed the gelding a few gulps of cold water before he urged it north at a walk.

It was almost noon when he crossed onto Chet Dodson's ranch land. Gabe could see the man's house, barn, and corrals about two miles off to the west. Remembering that he was supposed to tell an old man named Luther Rote that his employer was still alive, Gabe pointed the buckskin west.

Gabe crossed the tracks of shod horses and pulled his hat brim down against the sun, squinting hard, wondering if he might just be riding into trouble. There wasn't much doubt that if Caleb Burr thought Mace had killed Dobson, the powerful rancher would move to gobble up his fine ranch.

But when Gabe drew nearer, he saw another sight, one that put a whole new perspective on his thinking. There were three men all standing around a wooden cross and the mound of a fresh grave.

Gabe kept his rifle ready as he drove the buckboard

across Dodson's ranch yard and up to the three men.

The tallest of the three, a tall, ruggedly handsome man in his fifties, said, "You're Ella Porter's man, aren't you?"

Gabe nodded, his eyes taking in everything. "And who are you?"

"I'm John Paxton, this here is Pete Jakes, and that is Ed McDaniel. We all own ranches in this valley."

Gabe motioned toward the grave. "My guess is that would be Luther Rote you just buried."

"You got that right," Paxton said. "Poor devil was caught by a grizzly. Never had a chance. Wasn't something you'd care to see."

"I can imagine what he looked like," Gabe said, "because I've got Mace's body wrapped up in the back of this wagon. He was also killed by a bear."

The three ranchers all reacted with shock, then McDaniel said, "That ties it then, John! I'm going to sell out to Caleb for whatever I can get. I got a family to think of, and I've had to watch my wife age fifty years over these grizzly attacks."

"My wife is so scared," Jakes said, "she don't hardly eat anymore. She's just worn down to skin and bones by fear. And I'm at the end of my string too."

Only Paxton stood his ground. "I tell you," he argued, "something is dead wrong about all of this! That two-toed grizzly isn't normal! It acts against all the laws of nature."

"It's a demon!" Jakes swore. "And I for one am getting my wife and kids out of this accursed valley before we end up just the same as Mace and poor old Luther!"

Jakes and McDaniel, despite all of Paxton's arguments had made up their minds to quit and run. Gabe listened and when Paxton failed to calm his neighbors down, Gabe said, "I believe I can track that bear down and kill it."

"The hell you can!" Jakes swore. "We've hired men

and dogs before. Lots of 'em! And they either come up empty-handed or get killed. Mister, the best thing you can do is to ride out of this valley."

"Dodson and Mrs. Porter are still alive," Gabe said. "They both mean to fight for their ranches. I suspect they are hoping for your help."

Paxton's narrow face split into a grin. "Chet and Ella are alive?"

"They are."

"Well, where?"

Gabe hesitated. "I can't say just now. But I give you my word, they're alive and doing just fine. When the time is right, they'll be coming back."

McDaniel wasn't the least bit encouraged by this bit of news and said so. "I'm almighty glad to hear they're alive, mister, but that don't change the fact that Luther and Mace have both been killed by grizzly. And it don't change the fact that I'm selling out if Caleb Burr is still willing to buy."

"Me too," Jakes said.

"Well, I'm not!" John Paxton said with conviction. "We're going to kill that grizzly and end the trouble we've had with Burr one of these days. And when we do, this will be as fine a place to ranch as you'll ever find."

"He's right," Gabe said. "If you panic and sell now, you'll get practically nothing for your ranches. But if you wait until we've tracked down that grizzly and brought justice to this valley, you'll want to stay on."

Jakes and McDaniel exchanged furtive glances.

"What do you mean to do with the body you got in Ella's buckboard?" McDaniel asked.

"I'm going straight on to Caleb Burr's ranch. I figure that since Mace worked for him, he's the one that ought to do the burying."

"You do that," McDaniel warned, "and you'll never get off that man's ranch alive."

"I could use a little support," Gabe admitted. "Even as powerful as Burr is, I don't figure he could get away with shooting us all down."

"Don't you believe it!" Jakes exclaimed. "He'd just have his men say that we drew down on him and his gunnies first. Who'd there be to dispute that with us dead?"

Gabe expelled a deep breath. He figured maybe these men needed educating as to the reality of life in los Osos Valley.

"There's a showdown coming," he said. "I don't see any way to duck it. If I'm lucky, perhaps I'll find Burr at his bank in town and not even have to drive on to his ranch. If that's the case, there's no way that he could shoot us all. There would be too many witnesses."

Gabe paused and measured each of the three. Only Paxton looked like the kind of man who'd stand tall in a fight. The other two were less reliable, but their mere presence might be enough to hold Burr in check.

"How about you three just coming to Mesa with me? If Burr is in his office, maybe we can settle a few things right then and there. He won't have his gunmen along, or at least not all of them. We'll never have a better chance."

"To do what?" Jakes stormed.

Gabe scratched his stubbled cheeks. "Well," he said, "maybe to kill him if he's foolish enough to go for his gun first."

Before McDaniel and Jakes could protest, Paxton said, "I'll ride along with you. I've got too much money and life invested in my ranch to just hand it over to Caleb for a few cents on the dollar."

Paxton turned to his neighbors. "Pete, Ed, I sure wish you'd at least ride along with us into town. It'd be a fine show of support. If Chet and Ella were here now, they'd do it."

"Well, they aren't here!" Jakes swore. "And I got no wish to get shot down in Mesa."

Gabe had heard enough. Jakes and McDaniel were riddled with fear. They'd been living with the terror of grizzly and the fear of Caleb's hired guns too damn long to have any backbone remaining.

"I guess I'll be going on then," Gabe said. "But before I do, I want to say one thing. The grizzly that killed Mace and Luther isn't normal, and I got a hunch why and how to stop it."

"You want to tell us?" McDaniel stormed.

Gabe shook his head. "Nope." Then he snapped the lines across the buckskin's sweaty rump and drove away.

"Hang on!" Paxton yelled. "I'm coming along!"

Gabe kept the buckskin moving north. Paxton was a good man, but with just the two of them there was a fair possibility they would both be gunned down in the next hour.

CHAPTER TWELVE

When they neared Mesa, Gabe broke a long silence by saying, "Paxton, you don't have to go through with this. You can just turn around and ride on home."

"No, I can't," the man said. "Not and live with myself. This is my fight as much as anybody's—more than yours. Which leads me to ask why you're sticking your neck on the block."

"I'm doing it for Ella."

"That's what I figured," Paxton said. "You got sweet on her, didn't you?"

"A little. But when this trouble with Burr is over, I'll be moving on."

Paxton studied him, a question in his eyes. "Let's just suppose, for the sake of argument, that we are able to somehow settle the trouble with Caleb and even kill that damn demon bear. If all that happened, you'd be crazy to ride out of this valley. Ella has the best and the biggest ranch among us."

"I don't like punching cattle," Gabe said. "And I don't have any interest in logging or mining. So there's nothing for me here."

"But . . . but there's Ella herself!"

"I wouldn't be any good for her, John. And I've told her so. I think the man she ought to fix her eyes on is Chet Dodson."

"Chet?" Paxton's bushy eyebrows lifted with surprise. "Why, Chet's more afraid of Ella than he is of grizzly bears—almost."

Gabe chuckled. "It's a fact that he does get nervous around both. But the man is changing. Being around Ella all the time now, I think he's beginning to see that women don't bite."

Paxton rode on in silence for a few minutes. "My own feeling of the matter is that Dodson has had too many women chasin' *him*. It's kind of funny about that, you know. Here's a man petrified of the opposite sex, and that seems to attract them all the more! Some of the boys were talking about that just the other day. It doesn't make sense."

"Nothing about women makes sense," Gabe said. "And the more you try to figure them out, the more confounded your thinking becomes. Right now, figuring out how you and I are going to bring Caleb Burr down a peg or two is the most immediate problem I can call to mind."

"If you just up and shoot him, the townsfolk will lynch the both of us," Paxton said. "It's not that they're so fond of Caleb, it's just that he's the money man. Without him, Mesa would dry up and blow away. At least the mining and the sawmill would."

"I have no intention of killing him," Gabe said. "Not until I find and kill that two-toed grizzly bear."

"Are you saying you think that there's some connection?"

"I don't know," Gabe said quietly. "But I sure can't figure out why a grizzly would be so selective about whose cattle and horses it kills. Do you have any answers to that one?"

"No. But maybe it just doesn't consider Caleb's range a part of its territory."

Gabe shook his head. "And maybe Caleb has something to do with that," he said quietly.

When they arrived in town, Gabe drove right up in front of the bank and stepped down into the muddy street. There was a crowd already starting to gather behind the buckboard, everyone wondering who the man was wrapped up inside the blanket.

"Shall we tell them?" Paxton asked.

"No," Gabe said, easing his six-gun in its holster. "I think we'll keep it as a surprise for Caleb Burr." With that he headed for the bank's front door.

"You're really asking for it," Paxton muttered as he kept the crowd back from the frozen corpse in Ella's old buckboard.

When Gabe slammed inside the bank, the first thing he saw was a hired gunman sitting down smoking a cigarette in the lobby, guarding Caleb's office.

As Gabe started to brush past the man, the gunfighter raised to his feet and his hand went toward his gun. He wasn't sure that Gabe wasn't one of his boss' own men, so he was slow to react. Even so, there was no missing the challenge in his stance so Gabe took advantage of his indecision.

Long Rider's fist swung up from the knees and caught the gunman right at the apex of his rib cage, just below the sternum. The gunfighter's eyes bulged and his cheeks blew out. A moment later, he was grabbing for his solar plexus and collapsing to the polished wooden floor.

"Maybe I better take this, just in case," Gabe said, removing the man's gun while he was completely helpless.

Gabe entered the office and saw Caleb Burr reaching into his drawer. The gun which Gabe had just retrieved bucked in his fist, and a bullet splintered the wooden drawer less than an inch from Caleb's fingers. A splinter drove into the banker's fingers and the derringer he had just snatched spilled to the floor.

"Damn you!" Caleb cried, grabbing his lanced finger and grimacing with pain.

Gabe walked over and picked up the derringer. He glanced back at the gunfighter, still writhing on the floor and holding his midsection.

"Mr. Burr, we can do this the hard way or the easy way. Which will it be?"

"What the hell are you talking about?" the huge fat man cried. "I'll have you arrested, sentenced, and locked in a cell and the key will be thrown away!"

"Outside," Gabe growled as he jammed the six-gun into the fat man's ribs. "I got a little surprise package for you."

Caleb didn't want a surprise. He resisted, but when Gabe cocked the hammer of the six-gun and said, "I don't bluff," the man headed for the front door.

"What the—"

"Unwrap the body," Gabe hissed, shoving the gun barrel even harder into the man's blubber. "Unwrap him and take him home. He was on your payroll; that's the least he deserves."

When Caleb unwrapped the body, the blood drained from his normally rosy cheeks and he staggered back, mouth working in horror.

Gabe looked at the stunned crowd and said, "This man was hiding in Mrs. Ella Porter's stone corral, waiting to ambush us. But a grizzly got to him first. A grizzly that I have reason to believe is controlled by Caleb Burr."

"You're mad!" Caleb shouted.

"Am I? We'll see. I've got no proof, but I'm going to track that grizzly down and when I do, I think I'll have the answers to all the questions. And I'll have enough evidence to hang your fat hide."

Burr swallowed, still badly shaken by what he had just seen. "I'll see that you're arrested for this!"

"If you're talking about sending Marshal Flowers, you better warn him that I'll be hunting grizzly in the higher country. And somehow, I don't think he's the kind of a man who'll want to join in on that kind of fun."

"Damn you!" Burr screamed.

Gabe shoved the extra six-gun behind his waistband and latched onto Mace's boots. He dragged the corpse off the wagon and dumped it unceremoniously into the muddy, half-frozen street before he climbed back onto the buckboard.

"I'm going to bring you down, Burr. I'm going to track and kill that two-toed bear and, when I do, I'll have all the answers to this reign of terror that you've used to empty this valley down to just a handful of ranchers."

Burr swallowed noisily and began to shake with fury. "Mister, you're a walking dead man and you don't know it! I'll see that you're the one that's tracked down and killed like a rabid beast."

Gabe drew his own gun and pointed it at Caleb's chest. Bystanders shouted and most dove for cover as the barrel of Gabe's pistol shifted a fraction of an inch. When it spat fire, Caleb screamed and grabbed a bloodied ear.

"That's just so you'll know that if you send men after me, I'll come back and find you, Burr. You're too damn big and fat to hide. I'll find you and gun you down."

Gabe slapped the lines against the buckskin's haunches and the animal bolted away leaving the body of Mace in the mud and Caleb Burr bellowing with pain and outrage.

CHAPTER THIRTEEN

Caleb Burr was trembling with fury and pain as he called a war council behind the locked doors of his bank. Among the men present were four professional gunfighters and another half-dozen seasoned fighters who shot straight and would not hesitate to kill for money.

"I'm putting a bounty on that man's head," Caleb announced to the bank full of assembled hard cases.

The men grinned wolfishly.

"I'm offering a thousand dollars to the man who brings me his scalp. I'm also offering three hundred dollars each for the scalps of Chet Dodson and John Paxton. I want Ella Porter brought to me alive."

The gunfighter whom Gabe had left gasping for air and holding his solar plexus was the most eager. His name was B. D. Dooley, and he had killed seven men, most of them in the Arizona range wars, all of them in straight up gunfights instead of by ambush.

"Might be better to kill her, too. You don't need any witnesses," Dooley suggested.

"No," Caleb said, "she's to be kept alive and brought to my ranch house. I want that clearly understood by everyone. The woman isn't to be killed or hurt or in any way humiliated. I'll also pay three hundred dollars for her safe delivery. Is that clear to everyone?"

The roomful of men nodded, but Dooley swore, "Just as long as everyone understands that the bastard with the buckboard belongs to me."

"No!" Caleb swore, pounding his clenched fist down hard on the top of his desk, then grimacing in pain from his injured finger. "Dammit, no! Dooley, you already had your chance. Now, every man in this room has open season on the three men whose names I just mentioned."

Another gunfighter named Henry Horn who had earned his bloody reputation in Mexico and was renowned as a knife fighter, said, "Mr. Burr, you got any idea where we might find Dodson and that Porter woman?"

Caleb nodded with grim satisfaction. "As a matter of fact, I do. I've been told that Doc Landrum is hiding in an old log cabin up near Potter's Lake. It's about twenty miles from here. I'm sure some of you have been through there before."

"I have," a man said.

"Good!" Caleb's lips formed a thin smile. "There's a better than even chance that the Doc is helping Ella and Chet Dodson. So I'll tell you what, boys. Just for added incentive, I'll also put a three hundred dollar bounty on the Doc's head. That means if you get Dodson, Ella, and the Doc, there's nine hundred dollars in your pockets to spend."

"The hell with them! I know who I'm going after," Dooley swore, his gut still aching from the blow he'd taken. "Him and that Paxton fella."

"I think I'll go with you," Horn said, deciding that most of the men present would probably elect to ride up to Potter's Lake in search of Ella, the Doc, and Chet Dodson and that the bounty would be split too many ways to add up to very much for any one man.

Dooley wasn't pleased, but since his boss had made it damned clear that Gabe was fair game to anyone man enough to kill him, the gunfighter knew that he could not very well object.

"I'll be at my ranch," Caleb said gravely, "and I'll be waiting for scalps. Don't keep me waiting long."

The assembly knew that they had been dismissed and with the thought of so much money to be earned, they wasted no time in heading for their horses. This was a man-hunt, and the stakes were very much to everyone's liking.

Dooley was in the saddle and ready to ride in less than ten minutes. Henry Horn, with his huge bowie knife and the scars of many Mexican knife fights, was also one of the first ones ready to leave.

Three other men started to follow after them, but Dooley and Horn turned their horses around and the latter gun-fighter said, "I guess Dooley and I can handle this by ourselves without any more help."

One of the four dared to protest. "But Mr. Burr said it was open season! We want a part of that thousand dollars for the big man and the three hundred dollars for Paxton."

Dooley's hand slipped down near his gun butt and so did Horn's. "Two of us and four of you," Dooley said. "Good odds, don't you think, Horn?"

"I like them fine."

But the four men did not like the odds at all. Dooley and Horn were both deadly gunfighters, each with a reputation that no one could question.

"Reckon we'll join the others and ride up to Potter's Lake then," one of the four said. They all reined their horses around to join the larger bunch of men.

"Damn good idea," Horn said as he and Dooley turned their backs on Mesa and started following the wheel tracks of Ella Porter's old buckboard.

"You ever seen this fella before?" Horn asked.

"Nope. Not until the son of a bitch sucker punched me."

Horn rode along for almost a mile in silence. "He looks a lot like a fella called Long Rider. I heard of him down in Texas once."

When Horn did not elaborate, Dooley said impatiently, "Well, what the hell did you hear? Or are you going to keep it to yourself?"

"I hear he's got a twisted trigger finger on his right hand."

"Shit," Dooley swore, "I *saw* that! Tell me something I don't know."

Horn's eyes sparked with a cold anger, but his voice remained calm and even friendly. "He's supposed to be good with either hand, and it would be a bad mistake to think he can't draw because of that finger. A real bad mistake. He favors a cross draw with his left hand, but he also draws just fine with his right."

"He doesn't scare me one damn bit."

Horn shifted uneasily in his saddle. "He worries me some. It's been said that Long Rider can track like an Indian because he was raised by the Indians. He's supposed to be one dangerous son of a bitch when he's crossed."

Dooley shot his companion a look of contempt. "Maybe you're trying to talk yourself out of going after the man. If that's the case, you still got time to catch up with the crowd and ride up to Potter's Lake after an old hermit doctor, a wounded man, and a damned woman. Maybe fighting them would be more in keeping with your style anyway."

Horn's hand flashed to the knife at his side instead of his gun and the bowie's polished blade came to rest against Dooley's throat and brought him right up in his stirrups.

"Maybe," Horn said, spitting tobacco on Dooley's pants leg and watching a thin trickle of blood seep from his throat into his shirt collar, "maybe you should be a little more careful what you say to a man like me."

Dooley's mouth opened like a beached fish and his eyes were round with fright. Their horses were walking, and Dooley could feel that the blade of Horn's knife was every bit as sharp as a razor. One slip, or if either of their horses so much as stumbled, and his throat would be cut wide open.

"Nod your head if you understand me, Dooley."

Sweat beaded across Dooley's brow. "If I nod," he whispered, "you'll open my damned windpipe!"

Horn retracted his shining steel from Dooley's throat allowing him to nod his head.

"Good," Horn said pleasantly. "I didn't want to do that, but it seems to me that you needed to be taken down a peg or two. Everything I've ever heard about Long Rider tells me he is as dangerous as a rattlesnake in a bedroll. Now, I'm mighty quick with a six-gun, and I know you're also right sudden. But you have to understand one thing—nothing will get us killed any faster than underestimating this Long Rider fella, not to mention Paxton."

"Paxton's nothing!" Dooley choked, reaching up to touch his throat and seeing the smear of blood on his fingertips. "Dammit, you didn't need to cut me to make your point!"

"Oh yes I did," Horn said with a smile. "I seen too many men like you headed for a fall when they got too high and mighty an opinion of themselves. Now, I don't mind if you get killed, but if we face Long Rider and Paxton, I'm going to need your help. Afterward, if there are hard feelings over what just happened, we can settle our differences any way you please. But first, we stick together. Is that understood?"

"Of course it is!" Dooley swore, wanting to draw his gun and blow the man's brains all over the road. He would have done it too, except that Horn's bowie knife was still resting in his fist, and Dooley knew that the blade could reach his gut before he could draw and fire.

Horn acted so pleased by their understanding that he began to hum an old Mexican love song that he had learned down in the Mexican state of Chihuahua.

"I hear that you prefer to kill men with your knife," Dooley said a little farther down the road. "I find that hard to believe."

Horn stopped his humming and regarded his companion intently. "When I make love to a woman, I like to go inside of her as deep as I can. And when I kill a man, I like to do the same with the blade of my knife. Does that make any sense to you?"

Dooley took a real close look at Horn. The man's face had a long, jagged scar down one cheek, and he was missing an ear and a finger, the badges of knife fights hard won. Privately, Dooley was convinced that Horn was insane. Any man who enjoyed closing with another, tasting steel to deliver steel even deeper into flesh, *had* to be insane.

"Well," Horn said, "does it?"

"Sure," Dooley lied as he looked away and shivered.

CHAPTER FOURTEEN

Gabe was real quiet as he drove the buckboard south because his mind was preoccupied with the expected trouble that would follow him from Mesa. Of one thing he was very sure—Caleb Burr was going to send his hired gunmen to seek vengeance.

Paxton wasn't talking either, and Gabe supposed that the rancher was probably worried about his own hide and that of his family.

"You have a wife and children?" Gabe asked the man.

"I've a wife, but our children are grown up and moved on."

"I think you ought to leave as well," Gabe said, "at least for a while until this trouble blows over."

"It won't ever blow over," Paxton said bitterly. "There's only one way to change all of this and that's to kill Burr. But to do that, we'd have to take on his hired gunmen as well as half the town and a United States marshal."

Gabe was afraid that Paxton had it figured right. "That's why I think you ought to take your wife and leave the valley for a while."

"If I did that," Paxton said with a stubborn shake of his head, "when I came back, there'd be a couple of Burr's gunmen in my house, eating my beef and sleeping in my bed. No sir! Leaving is exactly what Burr is hoping I'll do."

"Your ranch isn't worth your life," Gabe said, "nor that of your missus."

Paxton's expression changed from anger to concern as they approached his home. "You're right about it not being worth Mrs. Paxton's life," he admitted. "It's just the principle of the thing. We love this valley despite all the hell we've been through. And other than Burr always coming after us and that goddamn two-toed bear you somehow think he controls, we'd be happy here."

Paxton was silent a few minutes waiting for Gabe to explain, but when he did not, Paxton blurted, "What did you mean when you told that crowd that you thought Caleb Burr was responsible for the grizzly attacks?"

"I mean I think he's found himself a grizzly bear trainer."

"What?" Paxton's rugged face reflected his shock and disbelief. "How the hell can you train a grizzly?"

"I don't know," Gabe confessed, "because no one I've ever known has tried. But maybe if you trapped a grizzly when it was a cub and raised it by hand, it might be possible."

Paxton shook his head. "I suppose it might be, but I'd sure have to see that to believe it. Every grizzly that I ever heard of was just naturally mean."

"So is the two-toed one," Gabe said. "He's a killer, but he might have a master who tells him who or what he can kill. There's no other explanation that I can think of for some of the things I've seen or why he attacks all but Caleb Burr's cattle and horses."

Paxton chewed on that all the way to his ranch house. When they rode into his yard, his wife, accompanied by a huge, long-haired black dog, hurried out to greet him with outstretched arms.

"I was worried to death about you!" she said, glancing at Long Rider as she hugged her man. "I saw Caleb's riders off in the distance and I was afraid that . . ."

"I know what you were afraid of," Paxton said, turning his wife toward Gabe and making the introductions. "Milly, this is Gabe Conrad. He's the man that is helping Ella."

Milly Paxton shook Gabe's hand very formally. "I am proud to know you," she said. "Ella is my best friend. She's got more pluck and spunk than all the rest of us ranch women combined."

"I doubt that," Gabe said. "Only a woman with courage would even attempt to live up here. But I've been telling your husband that I think he ought to take you on a little vacation to Santa Fe."

Milly turned to Paxton, her face suddenly alive with hope. "Oh, John, could we? Just for a while until things got better?"

"I can't leave," Paxton argued, "not with cattle and horses to feed and . . ."

"They'll take care of themselves for a week or so," Gabe said, "and by then this valley will either be safe for your return or else it will all belong to Burr. Either way, your lives are sure worth a lot more than the value of your livestock."

"He's right," Milly said. "John, let's go now!"

Paxton visibly struggled with this hard decision but finally, he nodded his head and Milly flung her arms around her husband's neck with joy.

"We'll leave first thing in the morning," Paxton said, gesturing at the dog. "He's a bear hunter. You want to keep him?"

Gabe studied the dog. It had the look of intelligence and great strength. He guessed the dog probably weighed well over a hundred pounds.

"What's his name?"

"Fidel. It means 'faithful' in Latin."

"Oh," Gabe said. "Has he ever cornered a bear?"

"Not yet."

"Then how do you know he would?"

"Because his parents both died fighting grizzly and every time one comes around, he about breaks his neck trying to get out into the forest and attack. But so far, I've kept him in close and on a line. At least alive he gives us some warning, even when he's confined to the inside of the cabin. Besides, I like him."

The dog wagged its tail, and Paxton reached down and scratched behind its ear.

"I don't want to get your pet dog killed," Gabe said, not sure if a dog would be a help or a hindrance.

"If he gets killed fighting a grizzly to save your life," Paxton said, "then that's what he was bred and raised to do."

Gabe thought about it another minute. He liked dogs and if he were going into the forest, it might be a big help to have a dog. "Is he a barker?"

"Nope. But if you're worried he might give your presence away, I've got a muzzle that you can put on him."

"No muzzle," Gabe said, patting the dog on the head. "All right, I think he might be a help."

"Good!" Paxton was obviously relieved. "You won't regret keeping him, though he eats more than a horse. He'll come when you call. I've taught him well. But it'll be tough for us both saying good-bye to him in the morning."

"Yes, it will," Milly seconded.

But Gabe shook his head. "I think you'd better leave within the hour for Santa Fe."

"And leave you here alone?"

"I won't stay here," Gabe explained. "I'll go to Ella's ranch tonight then strike out in the morning hunting that grizzly."

The worried look on Paxton's face deepened. "Listen, I've got an old buffalo rifle in the cabin. It'll blow a hole through a bear as big around as your fist. There's no doubt that it would stop a grizzly dead in its tracks."

"I think I'll accept your offer," Gabe said, "and then you'd best be on your way."

It was nearly sunset when the Paxtons had their wagon loaded and were ready to leave.

"How will we know whether or not to come back?" Paxton said, by now as resigned as his wife to the fact that everything he'd worked for rested on the hope that Gabe Conrad could somehow kill the grizzly and bring Caleb Burr to a long overdue justice.

"Just give yourself a week or two and keep your ear to the ground."

"I don't even know why you're doing this," Paxton said. "I mean, you don't own anything here. There's nothing at stake for you to risk your life fighting over."

"Yes, there is," Gabe said. "It's like you said, it's the principle of the thing."

Milly reached across her husband's lap and stretched out her hand which Gabe took in farewell. "You are a good man, Mr. Conrad. A fine man. But I fear for your life."

"I'm not afraid of death," Gabe said. "I was raised to believe that it is just the passing of one state into the next. Besides, with Fidel's help, I think we are going to be just fine."

Milly was cheered to hear these encouraging words. "Yes, and even though he has never fought a grizzly, we are sure that he will offer his own life to save that of a friend. Treat him well, and he will reward you with bravery and loyalty."

"I will," Gabe promised.

When their wagon was loaded, Paxton shook Gabe's hand. "I don't feel right about leaving you to fight my battle."

"Sometimes the hardest thing to do is to walk away from a fight," Gabe said. "That's what you're doing now for the sake of your wife."

Paxton opened his mouth to say something, then thought better of it and nodded.

"Ten days to two weeks. If we don't hear anything after that . . ."

"Then give it a few more weeks," Gabe suggested.

Paxton frowned but said nothing as he took his lines and slapped them across the rump of his team and drove away quickly. Milly looked back over her shoulder at the Paxton cabin, and the sadness in her expression told Gabe that she never expected to see their home again.

On a stout rope leash, Fidel whined softly to see the Paxtons roll away.

"With luck," Gabe said as he knelt and scratched the dog's huge head, "they'll be back home before the first big snowfall."

In reply, Fidel licked Gabe's hand and made a commendable attempt to wag his thick tail.

"I think," Gabe said, "that you and I are going to make a pretty decent team."

CHAPTER FIFTEEN

Gabe would have liked to have taken the Paxtons up on their offer to sleep in their warm cabin, but he figured that would not be a very smart thing to do given that Burr's henchmen would be out for his hide.

"I'm afraid we're going to have to rough it a little," Gabe explained to the huge dog who sat upright on the buckboard seat beside him. "I don't know what kind of a life you've had until now, but things are going to get bumpy for a while."

Fidel whined softly, his great brown eyes smiling happily as Gabe ruffled the fur on his collar.

It was nearly midnight before he arrived at Ella's ranch. The sky was ablaze with glittering stars as Gabe unhitched his weary buckskin and turned it free in the hay barn.

"Eat your fill," he said. "You've earned it."

Gabe was dead tired, but there was much to be done yet in preparation for leaving so he resisted the impulse to sleep and lowered a quarter of beef from the barn's rafters. With Fidel licking his chops, Gabe cut off thick slabs of the hindquarter, feeding the dog plenty before hauling the meat back to the cabin. For the next hour, he cooked beef, then gorged himself knowing that it might be a day or two before he and the dog had time to eat well again.

What he and Fidel did not eat, Gabe packed into his saddlebags. It was Long Rider's opinion that a man never knew how long he might be out on a bear hunt, and it made things easier when he wasn't weakened by starvation.

"If we run out of beef, I guess I'll just have to shoot that two-toed bear and we'll eat a hunk of him, huh Fidel?" Gabe said with a weary smile.

The dog thumped its thick tail down hard on the floor and licked its chops. The beast had eaten at least five pounds of raw meat and still looked hungry.

There were only a few hours left before dawn when Gabe and Fidel made their way back out to the barn. Once inside, Gabe latched the barn door and even dragged a wagon wheel up against it to guard against any surprise visitors. His body was crying for rest and he knew that he'd be a much better man with even a couple hours of sleep.

"I expect this isn't necessary," he said to the dog. "If Burr's men were to show up, you'd let me hear about it, wouldn't you?"

Again, Fidel's big black tail wagged.

"Good boy," Gabe said as he eased down on a pile of hay and closed his eyes thinking how tomorrow was bound to be a very eventful day. He'd be hunting the killer grizzly, and Burr's gunmen would be hunting him. That would make things damned exciting, Gabe thought as he drifted off to sleep.

Two hours after daybreak, Fidel woke Gabe with a low, warning rumble. Long Rider bolted upright with his gun clenched in his fist.

"Are they here already?" he asked, knuckling the sleep from his eyes.

Fidel's continued growl was all the answer that Gabe needed. He yanked on his boots and crept over to the barn door. Peering through the crack between the two swinging doors, he saw two gunmen dismount out by the corral and tie their horses before they began stalking Ella's cabin. Gabe's lips formed a hard line. He knew that the gunmen would rush the cabin in the next few minutes, and, when they didn't find him inside, they'd head for this hay barn.

Gabe carefully considered his next move. He figured that, if he played things right, he could kill both these men and then go bear hunting. But the thing of it was, he did not like the idea of ambushing the pair from cover. It wasn't his style, but if he faced them, then *he* might be the one that was killed. Gabe couldn't afford to die. If he went down in a hail of bullets, then he'd have done nothing to change the sad course of events in this valley. The killer grizzly would continue to raid and Caleb Burr would soon eliminate the last of his opposition.

"It's not worth the risk yet," he muttered to himself. "I've *got* to find that two-toed bear and take care of it first. After that, I'll settle with Burr and whoever else the man sends after my hide."

Decision made, Gabe prepared to escape. He grabbed his bridle and jammed the bit between the gelding's teeth. Then he shook out his saddle blanket and quickly saddled the buckskin who had not stopped eating since he'd turned it loose the night before. With stiff, cold hands, Gabe lashed his bedroll and saddlebags behind his cantle. Lastly, he stuffed the beefsteak he'd cooked the night before into his saddlebags.

Satisfied that he was ready, Gabe pulled the wagon wheel away from the barn door, then picked up the loaded buffalo rifle that Paxton had loaned him and tied it to his saddle horn before he mounted and drew his six-gun. The buckskin stomped nervously and Fidel's growl deepened.

"Now don't you go playing hero," Gabe told the dog. "I want you to just follow me. You understand?"

In answer, Fidel wagged his tail.

Taking that as a signal, Gabe spurred the buckskin hard enough to send it crashing into the barn doors, knocking them wide open as Gabe and Fidel burst outside.

Horn and Dooley were caught flat-footed in surprise and both dived for cover as Gabe's bullets swarmed around them. By the time they recovered, Gabe, Fidel, and the buckskin had crossed the yard and were driving their two saddle horses off down the valley.

"Son of a bitch!" Dooley screamed. "I'll kill him for that!"

But Horn's reaction was altogether different. A slow grin spread across his knife-scarred face as he watched the man, dog, and horses race away until they were nothing but specks on the horizon.

"What the hell are you grinning about?" Dooley cried in anger.

"I don't know," Horn said. "I guess I'm smiling because Long Rider didn't decide to stick his rifle through some crack in that barn and open fire on us. Seems like a reason worth smiling for, don't you think?"

Dooley was taken aback. What Horn said made sense. Relaxing, he said, "So why do you suppose he didn't try to ambush us from the barn?"

Horn shrugged his broad shoulders. "I don't rightly know. Either one of us would, but Long Rider is a different breed of cat. In any case, we're damn lucky to be alive."

"Yeah, well, we got a long walk ahead, and I don't think that's anything to smile about."

Horn's grin faded. "I guess not. However, it's my opinion that walkin' never killed a man."

"Shit!" Dooley swore. "This is the second time that Indian-lovin' son of a bitch has turned the tables on me. And I tell you one thing, I'd be hunting him even if I had to do it for free!"

"I sure as hell wouldn't," Horn said. "Long Rider is just too damn dangerous. And my guess is that we're going to earn every cent of that thousand dollar reward that Caleb Burr put on his hide."

Horn brushed himself off and, without further discussion, started walking after their horses. After a moment, Dooley swore and hurried to catch up with him.

CHAPTER SIXTEEN

Ella stared out the window of Doc Landrum's cabin and watched the fading afternoon sun color the western mountaintops.

She wondered if Gabe was still alive and if Caleb Burr had yet taken over her ranch. Doc had gone off earlier in the day, riding Chet's mule, Sarah, claiming that he had "business" to take care of and that he would not return until much later.

Ella turned to see Chet Dodson feeding the stove, his long, handsome face peaceful and reflective in the firelight. She and Chet had spent every waking hour together since arriving at this cabin, and Ella had discovered, much to her surprise, that she was strongly attracted to the young bachelor.

For his own part, being forced to live so closely with a pretty young woman tending his wound had caused a profound change in Chet Dodson as well. Chet had never been around women, and he had supposed them to be mysterious, totally different than men in every way. To his surprise, Ella was not so different at all. She had the same strongly held views as his own on cattle and horses. She also loved los Osos Valley and hated Caleb Burr, and most important of all, she was determined to fight for her ranch land.

With those important things in common, the two of them had spent hours discussing their hopes and fears, and somewhere along the way, Chet had forgotten to be shy around a woman.

"What you thinking about?" he asked quietly, noting her faraway expression.

"I was wondering about the Doc," she answered, "wondering where he would go on such a bitterly cold day in these high mountains."

"Maybe he has a Ute squaw or a white woman hidden away in some cabin just like this one."

"Doc Landrum?"

"Sure. Just because he doesn't like men a whole lot, that doesn't mean he feels the same way about women. I've noticed that he is mighty partial to you, Ella."

Ella laughed. "The Doc once fixed my broken arm. I took a bad spill from a bronc. Rumor has it that you once saved his life. Is that true?"

Chet nodded his head. "I guess so."

Ella waited for some explanation and, when it didn't come, she said, "Aren't you going to tell me about it?"

"Okay, but it wasn't such a big thing. One day I heard the Doc's mule brayin' like crazy up by the trees not too far above my ranch. I decided that maybe I ought to go see what was wrong."

"How did you know anything was wrong?"

Chet was silent for a moment, then said, "I could just tell by the sound of the mule that it was in trouble. So I grabbed a rifle and jumped on a horse. By the time I reached the mule, I saw that a grizzly bear was trying to bring her down and had clawed up her hindquarter pretty bad. The grizzly was young and smallish but madder than a teased snake. Had it been a big bear, it would have broken that mule's neck with a single swipe of its paw."

"So what did you do?"

"I was pretty scared," Chet admitted. "I knew that I had to get off my horse if I was going to shoot straight but that, if I did, a wounded bear might attack me."

"Where was the Doc?"

"He was out cold under the mule." Chet shook his head. "It was like the mule was trying to protect him from that bear. I believed she was then, and I believe it now. A horse would have run away faster'n a scalded cat, but not that mule. Mules are loyal. Like my Sarah is."

Ella leaned forward. "So you shot the grizzly and saved the Doc's life. Is that it?"

"Pretty much," Chet admitted. "But I didn't do it the easy way. I was so nervous my first shot went a foot wide and just hit that bear in the left shoulder. It came for me real fast, and I barely got off two more rounds before it knocked me about ten feet down the mountainside and then came to finish me off."

"How did you survive?"

"I was lucky. I landed in the middle of some rocks and they slowed the bear down. Somehow, I'd kept ahold of my six-gun, and I still had three rounds left. When the bear landed on me and went for my throat, I jammed the gun into its throat instead and emptied my gun, killing it before it killed me first."

"I've seen your scars," Ella said, "and I figured that you'd done something brave like that. No wonder the Doc was so worried when Gabe brought you up here."

"Next to old Luther Rote, the Doc is my best friend. Sometimes he'd even come down to our ranch and have a meal and a couple glasses of whiskey with us on a summer's evening." Chet smiled and got a faraway look in his eyes. "You may not believe this, Ella, but the Doc has a real fine sense of humor. He could make old Luther and me laugh until our sides were ready to split."

Watching Chet smile, Ella could feel her heart melt. The man was so innocent and boyishly naive, yet, Ella recalled how her own husband had once remarked that it was Chet Dodson that all the other small ranchers had most respected as a man first and then as a rancher.

Ella came over to stand beside Chet who looked at her with such intensity that it made her shiver. "Chet, can I ask you a very personal question?"

He gulped noisily and nodded his head.

"How come you never took a wife and fathered a brood of tall, handsome children? Don't you like women?"

He blushed and Ella thought he was going to turn away from her, but instead he took a deep breath and said, "I like women so much they've always scared me."

"I don't understand that."

"I don't either," he admitted. "I just find that I get tongue-tied and stutter when I try to speak to a pretty woman."

"Do you think I'm pretty?"

He took a deep breath. "You're more than pretty," he said, "you're plain beautiful."

Ella placed her hands on his shoulders. "Thank you for saying that. And I don't notice you stuttering now."

"You're . . . you're different," he said quickly. "And maybe it's because we've gotten to know each other these last few days. But you're different than all the others."

"And so are you," she told him, closing her eyes and kissing his mouth very tenderly.

When Ella opened her eyes, he was staring at her, eyes glazed with desire and he said, "Why'd you do that? Why'd you kiss me?"

"Because I wanted to," she said. "I think I even *needed* to kiss you, Chet."

"But . . . but I thought that you and Long Rider were . . ."

"I did, too," she said, "but Gabe isn't a marrying man. He'll never settle down with one woman. He doesn't even like cattle. I intend to stay in this valley, Chet. I want to keep my ranch and get remarried and raise strong children."

Chet gulped.

Ella smiled and kissed him again. "Do you want to stay and raise a family here?"

"Well, I . . . I never wanted to ranch anyplace else, but as for raising a family, well, I . . ."

Chet could not go on. His cheeks were aflame, and Ella could feel him trembling. "I don't understand," she whispered in his ear, "how a man like you could be so brave as to be willing to stand up to Caleb Burr and his gunfighters as well as a grizzly, but still feel so frightened over a woman who does not weigh one hundred and twenty-five pounds wet and who couldn't hurt you even if she tried."

"I don't understand it either," Chet confessed, "but that's the way I am."

Ella stepped back and surveyed him closely. "I thought I was in love with Edgar while he was alive, and then Gabe came along and I fell in love with him, too. But now . . . now I feel like you're the man that I've been waiting for all my life. We could get married, combine our ranches and prosper. We could raise a family and help turn this valley into a good place to live."

"And we could also get ourselves killed if we aren't careful," Chet said. "Burr will put a bounty on my head, if he hasn't already."

"I'm willing to bet that we find a way to whip him and break his stranglehold on the valley," Ella said. "And I'm thinking that you and I should make love."

"What?"

Chet would have jumped back and raced out of the cabin but Ella clung to him and, after a moment, he calmed down and stopped struggling.

"What is the matter?" she asked. "Haven't you ever made love to a woman?"

He couldn't answer so he shook his head, then summoned up enough nerve to say, "And I'm afraid I'd make a terrible botch of it if we tried."

Ella stepped back and unbuttoned her man's shirt.

"Oh geeze," Chet whispered, staring wide-eyed.

"You can do it," Ella said with encouragement as she moved toward him and took his hands.

After a long moment, she felt his fingertips touch her skin, and although they were rough from ranch work, he used them gently and Ella sighed with pleasure.

"You're doing just fine," she breathed.

CHAPTER SEVENTEEN

Gabe drove the riderless horses he'd captured from Horn and Dooley a good five miles before he reined into the forest and headed for Doc Landrum's cabin. The Doc, Ella, and Chet Dodson all needed to be warned that trouble was on its way.

He pushed the buckskin hard, not following any particular trail but certain of his bearings. At the end of several hours, the gelding was heaving with exhaustion. Vapor clouds were pulsing from its distended nostrils and even Fidel was panting with his steaming tongue hanging out.

"All right," Gabe said when the dog gazed up at him with questioning eyes. "We're almost at the summit and can't be more than four or five miles from Doc's cabin. We'll take a quick breather."

Gabe dismounted and tied the gelding to a pine tree. He scaled a boulder and now had a clear view of the valley far below.

Long Rider studied the valley. He did not know for sure that gunmen would be coming up to kill or capture Ella and Chet, but he suspected as much. And if they were, then . . .

He stiffened when he saw a glint of metal in the forest

trees less than a mile away. Gabe drew in a sharp breath. Yes, there it was again!

He strained to see what appeared to be at least eight riders moving in single file up the mountain. "It's a good thing we didn't sleep in this morning," Gabe said to the dog at his side, "and I'm afraid that we'll be cutting our rest stop short."

The buckskin was cranky and its flanks were still moving in and out as it sought to catch its breath when Gabe checked his cinch and then remounted. He continued on up the mountainside with renewed urgency.

Twenty minutes later, he topped the ridge and saw Potter's Lake off in the distance. He figured that he'd have just about enough time to reach the cabin before Burr's gunmen came over this same high divide. As for what he would do when he arrived at the cabin, well, that would depend on Doc, Chet, and Ella. They could run, or they could make a stand at Potter's Lake. Gabe was for making a stand because he'd already been running all day, and if the Doc and Ella both had rifles, then the odds were not all that long anymore.

"What about you, Fidel?" he asked the panting dog. "I'll bet you're ready to stand and fight, too."

Fidel, big tongue lolling out of the corner of his mouth, seemed to grin as his tail brushed the hard, cold ground.

"Yeah," Gabe said, "I can tell that you were made to fight and not run. Well, my friend, I kind of like to think I was born to do the same."

Gabe pushed his gelding hard down to the cabin and was surprised that he didn't hear Sarah hee-hawing an alarm until he rode into the yard and saw that Chet's mule was gone even though Ella's dapple was still in the corral.

Gabe dismounted, glancing over his shoulder to see if

Burr's men were yet in view and discovering that they were, though still a long, long way off.

He tied his sweaty gelding to Doc's rickety hitch rail and hurried into the cabin to discover, to his great surprise, Chet and Ella frantically making love on a bearskin rug that they'd spread on the floor beside the stove.

"Gabe!" Ella cried, struggling to push Chet off faster than he was already trying to scramble.

Gabe shook his head and turned away saying, "Chet, good to see that you're feeling so frisky again because we've got company coming."

Chet was so mortified that he stammered, "Who . . . who else for cripes sakes!"

"Oh, about eight hired guns. I reckon they're after a bounty placed on all of us. So you two lovebirds had better get dressed in a real hurry."

Gabe listened to them scramble around grabbing clothes for a moment, then he went out to his horse and retrieved the buffalo rifle and his Winchester from its saddle boot.

Madly buttoning up the front of his pants and with his holster and six-gun in his hand, Chet rushed outside. He was shirtless and his face was flushed with exertion. Under different circumstances, he would have been too embarrassed to even look Gabe in the eye, but now, there was no time for anything but trying to figure out how to stay alive.

"How many?"

"Looks like eight," Gabe said.

"Do you want to fight or run?"

"Well," Gabe said thoughtfully, "seeing as how my horse is altogether played out and that dapple of Ella's is slower than cold maple syrup, I don't think we've much choice but to stand and fight."

"The odds aren't good," Chet said, watching the riders still a good two miles away as they hurried down a rocky slope moving single file toward the lake.

"You're right about that," Gabe said, "but maybe we can whittle them down some."

"How?" Ella demanded, coming out tucking her man's shirt into her pants and avoiding Gabe's eyes.

"I think Chet and I will go meet them at a rocky point on the slope where they can't run or hide. If we're good, we ought to be able to shorten the odds."

"I want to come, too," Ella demanded.

"All right," Gabe said, "but only part way. You can back up our retreat. There's no chance we can take them all on, and when we fall back, we'll need you to cover us. Chet, get your rifle. I'll bridle Ella's dapple mare. There isn't time to saddle her, but we won't be riding far."

When Gabe started toward the corral, Ella rushed after him. "Gabe," she cried, "I'm sorry about what you saw just now!"

"I'm not," he said, not slowing down as he grabbed Ella's bridle off a post and ducked through the split rail fencing.

"But I don't think you understand!" Ella pleaded. "I . . ."

Gabe jammed the bit into the dapple's mouth. "Ella, I seen all I needed to understand that you have found a good man who'll marry you. That's more than I'd have done. So instead of giving me some lame explanation, why don't you just make things up to me by doing as I say and helping us take on all those jaspers that are coming for our scalps."

Ella's lips formed a tight line and she dipped her head, then turned and ran for the cabin and a rifle.

In less than three minutes, they were mounted and riding hard through the forest to intercept the bounty hunters. Chet and Ella were mounted double on the mare and Gabe was back on his exhausted buckskin gelding with Fidel right on his heels.

The gelding was badly played out, but at least it had

managed to get a short breather at the Doc's cabin. Even so, at this high altitude, it was blowing hard within a mile and so Gabe knew that he could not run it far before the animal would quit on him. Chet and Ella wouldn't be able to go much farther on that dapple mare.

"There it is!" Gabe shouted. "Ella, you stay back in those trees with a rifle and cover our retreat!"

Ella jumped off the horse and levered a shell into the Winchester she carried. "Just don't get in my line of fire!" she called as Gabe and Chet raced ahead.

When Gabe came to the spot that he figured would offer them the best cover and vantage point, he jumped off his gelding, tied it behind a big pine tree, and raced up to take his firing position, the buffalo rifle in one fist, his Winchester in the other. Chet and big Fidel were right behind him.

"There they are," Gabe said, pointing. "I'll take the lead rider with this buffalo rifle, you take the second man, and we'll alternate."

"We won't get no four apiece, that's for damn sure," Chet said, "but we'll cut them down to a respectable number."

Gabe nodded in agreement. He stretched out full on the ground and rested the buffalo rifle across a small rock. Then, he drew a bead on the lead rider's shoulder because seriously wounding the enemy in this case would be every bit as effective as killing and maybe even more so because a man howling in pain could easily demoralize his companions.

"Here we go," Long Rider whispered as he squeezed the trigger.

The buffalo rifle roared like a cannon and kicked worse than a mule. A huge cloud of white smoke erupted from its muzzle, and when Gabe squinted through it, he saw the lead rider's horse galloping into the forest and its owner laid out on the shale with a splash of red in the center of his chest.

"Damn thing shoots a little to the right," Gabe said, pushing the heavy rifle aside and snatching up his Winchester.

"Here they come!" Chet yelled.

The riders had scattered off the trail, then regrouped and were charging forward, trying to reach the trees where they would be safe. Gabe and Chet would have done exactly the same in their place. But before their enemies could reach cover, two more horses were running free and riderless.

"What will they do now?" Chet asked.

"Regroup and try to flank us." Gabe inched back and then when he felt he was out of sight, he crouched and rushed to his horse.

Fidel whined softly and Gabe patted the dog's head and said, "Your time will come to fight, but this isn't it. You just stay low and keep out of their rifle sights. I'm going to need you later."

Fidel's thick tail wagged hopefully.

Gabe and Chet mounted up and raced back toward Ella and the lakeside cabin.

"There's five left of them and still three of us," Gabe said as they barricaded themselves in the cabin with Fidel, "and those odds don't seem so bad."

"Doc is supposed to show up today sometime," Ella said. "Maybe he's already heard the gunfire and is out there right now."

"If he is," Gabe said, peering out through one of the gun holes that Doc had conveniently placed on all four walls, "he can show up anytime before dark because that's when they'll rush this cabin."

"I don't see how we can keep them out," Ella said. "And the first thing they'll do is fire the roof."

"I'm afraid that you're right," Gabe said.

"So what do we do?"

Gabe thought about it for a minute while he kept a sharp watch through the gun hole. When he saw movement in the trees, he unleashed a quick bullet, knowing as he pulled the trigger that he would miss but wanting those outside to be aware that no one was going to fall asleep in the cabin, that taking it was going to be costly.

Gabe turned back to the couple watching him, anxious for some plan of action. "I guess that Fidel and I are going to sneak outside and pay them a visit as soon as it gets dark."

"No!" Ella cried. "You wouldn't stand a chance out there alone."

Gabe snapped his fingers and the huge black dog trotted over to his side, tail whacking the wall.

"I won't be alone," he said. "And if we get in a real tight spot, then we can always come running back here."

"I don't like it," Chet said. "I think we ought to all stay together."

"And get roasted?" Gabe shook his head. "No thanks."

Ella and Chet exchanged worried glances while Gabe watched the last glimpse of daylight vanishing behind the western mountains.

It was going to be a very interesting night.

CHAPTER EIGHTEEN

Long Rider waited until full darkness had descended and then he fashioned a combination leash and muzzle out of a strip of leather for Fidel.

"Is that really necessary?" Ella asked.

"I don't know," Gabe said, "but if he were to start barking out there, he could get both of us shot in a hell of a hurry."

Chet scowled. "I still think I should go along with you."

"No," Gabe said. "If we are shot, it will be up to you to save Ella. You'd have to get her out of this cabin before they torched it to the ground, then use the cover of darkness to escape."

Ella reached up on her toes and kissed Long Rider's cheek. "You be careful."

"Sure," he told her as he moved to the door with Fidel.

He was lucky in that there was almost no moon and enough clouds to block out much of the starlight. Gabe took a deep breath, then rushed outside along the front of the cabin leading Fidel and expecting a fusillade of bullets that never came. When he rounded the corner of the cabin, he headed into the trees, his six-gun clenched in his big fist, hearing a low, ominous rumble in Fidel's throat.

Once they were in the trees the darkness was almost total, and when the big dog began to strain forward, Gabe decided that he might as well make use of the animal's superior night vision so he gave Fidel his lead. Unfortunately, the huge dog didn't care about low-hanging tree branches as they rushed forward so Gabe was clotheslined twice. But he survived until suddenly Fidel gathered himself and jumped high into the darkness. Gabe's arm was almost torn from its socket.

"Get him off of me!" a man screamed as he thrashed about on the ground with Fidel snarling at his throat. "Get him off me!"

Fumbling in the darkness, Gabe managed to find the dog's leash, but before pulling him off the terror-filled gunman, he used his own pistol to knock the man out cold.

"Hey, Luke!" a man called out of the darkness.

"Get him!" Gabe hissed, releasing the dog.

"What the—ahhh! Help!"

Gabe staggered blindly forward operating from hearing instead of sight.

"Fidel!" he shouted. "Come here!"

A few seconds later, the dog banged into his leg, knocked him down, and then lapped at his face.

Gabe quickly tied the leash around the dog's neck, hearing the confused shouts of his enemies. A muzzle flash winked in the darkness and was quickly accompanied by several more.

"Over there!" a man cried. "He's got a dog with him!"

"Kill them both!" another man bellowed.

Overhead, the clouds parted and starlight illuminated the forest. Seeing a man lift his six-gun, Gabe unleashed a bullet of his own. The bounty hunter crashed over a fallen log and lay still.

A bullet plucked at Gabe's coat as he dove for the cover of the brush, allowing Fidel to break free. A moment later, there was another gunshot, and Gabe heard the dog yelp in pain before he heard the huge dog bore his enemy down and snarl viciously in the night.

Gabe got up and ran to Fidel, pulling him off a man who then scrambled to his feet and bolted off through the forest. For a moment, Gabe almost set Fidel after him, but he changed his mind and kept the dog under control.

"Gabe, look out!" a voice cried somewhere in the trees behind him.

Instinctively, Gabe jumped at the dog, pulling it down as two bullets passed just inches over his head. He tried to twist around and bring his gun to bear on his ambusher, but Chet's gun banged twice, sending Gabe's ambusher twisting to the earth where he quivered then lay still in death.

"Gabe!" Ella cried, dropping her rifle and coming out from cover. "Are you all right?"

"A little nicked up," he said, running his hands over Fidel's rough coat until he felt the wetness of blood. "But the dog took a bullet."

"Let's get him into the cabin where we can have a look at him," Chet said.

A few minutes later, they were back inside. By lamplight, they inspected Fidel's thick coat until Gabe said, "There! He took a bullet across the neck."

"Let me see," Ella said, running her fingers through the dog's coat as she traced the wound. "It feels like the bullet passed through cleanly."

Gabe examined the wound while Fidel lay still between them, seeming to enjoy all the attention. "You're right," he said at last, "but he's still bleeding pretty heavily."

"I'll get some bandages," Ella said, jumping to her feet.

In ten minutes, they had what looked like a big, white, horse collar wrapped around Fidel's neck. They were just finishing up when the door to the cabin burst open and Doc jumped inside with a sawed-off shotgun clenched in his fists. He looked wild and crazy enough to Gabe to shoot first and ask questions later.

"What happened?" he demanded, lowering the shotgun.

"We were attacked, and if it hadn't been for this dog, it would have been rough sledding," Gabe said.

Doc Landrum propped up his rifle beside the door and marched over to the dog. With a grunt of apparent disgust, he unwrapped the bandages that Ella had so carefully supplied and then he reexamined Fidel's gunshot wound.

"Humph!" he snorted, waddling over to his medical bag and extracting a pair of scissors which he used to cut away the dog's blood-matted hair.

"Hold that lantern up here close so that I can see better," he ordered.

The Doc studied the bullet wound for several minutes, then he returned to his medical bag for some salve. Scooping up a gob of it, he quickly applied the medicine to the dog's wound and then studied Fidel with a critical eye.

"Damn handsome animal, ain't he?" he said at last. "Wonder if John Paxton would sell him to me."

"You'd have a hell of a time finding him to ask," Gabe said, "because I told Paxton to take his wife and leave the valley until things were settled one way or the other."

The doctor put the salve away and warmed his hands by the stove, rubbing them together briskly. "This trouble isn't going to end until Caleb Burr and that killer grizzly bear are dead. The three of you know that as well as I do."

"So what are you suggesting?" Gabe asked.

"I'm suggesting it might be easier to start with the bear first. He'll be about ready to hibernate. We'll either get him now or the chance is lost until next spring."

Gabe agreed. "Paxton said that this dog of his would help me find that two-toed killer. I'll start searching for the grizzly's tracks first thing tomorrow morning."

"You don't need to track him," the Doc said, "because I think I know where he can be found."

Ella, Chet, and Gabe all blinked with surprise. The Doc waited a moment, seeming to enjoy the suspense.

"Well?" Ella demanded with anger and impatience. "Are you going to tell us or not?"

Doc continued to rub his hands together over the hot stove. "The reason I left this cabin was to go hunt that bear. Like Gabe, I knew that something wasn't right—grizzly don't pick and choose whose cattle or horses they attack."

"What are you driving at?" Gabe asked.

"I once knew a man named Dane who claimed he had lived with ferocious bears in Scandinavia and that he had a special power over them. He was a huge fella, rough, and always dangerous when drunk, which was most of the time. He was a logger years ago but got to be so vicious and quarrelsome that everyone was afraid to be around him. So he went off into the woods and became a hunter and a trapper."

Gabe rubbed his whiskered chin. "So what are you trying to tell us? That maybe this Dane fella has somehow figured out a way to control the two-toed bear?"

"I'd say that there was a real good chance of it," Doc replied.

"Where can we find him?"

"That's the hard part," Doc said. "You see, I been tromping around the country where he used to be just looking for signs of him and that bear."

"And you found something?" Gabe said.

"Exactly," Doc Landrum answered. "I located Dane's tracks leading up toward a box canyon about twenty miles north of here."

"What about the grizzly? Did you find his tracks as well?" Gabe asked.

"I did."

Gabe expelled a deep breath of relief. "That's it then," he said. "I'll head for that box canyon at first light."

"Now wait a minute!" Chet interrupted. "I figure to come along, too!"

"And so do I," Ella told him. "Are you forgetting that that bear killed my husband! If you expect me to just stay here, you can just think again."

Gabe tried to stare them down, but it was no use. "All right," he said with resignation. "We'll all go bear hunting tomorrow at first light."

"Not *all* of us," Doc said, trudging off to his bed where he sat down heavily. "I'm worn down to a nubbin. But I'll draw you a map to that box canyon if you'll bring over my writing materials."

"What are you going to do while we're gone?" Chet asked, thinking about how more of Caleb Burr's bounty hunters might still be prowling about these mountains.

"Sleep and read in the peace and quiet of my own damn company," Landrum snapped.

Gabe knew better than to object. Besides, Doc looked to be exhausted. The man was far too old and slow to be tromping back out into the woods again so soon.

"And I'll be here," Doc said, scribbling out a map centered by Potter's Lake, "in case there's anything left of any of you that survives."

They were ready to leave at first light. The dapple and buckskin were saddled and even though they needed a third animal, they decided to leave Chet's Sarah behind, thinking her braying might give them away. Gabe insisted that the cantankerous old doctor go over his map one more time so that there would be no mistakes.

"It's all there in front of your eyes, dammit!" Doc swore. "Just follow my map!"

"This Dane fella, what does he look like?"

"He's about six-and-a-half-feet tall with blond hair and blue eyes. And if he sees you before you see him, you'll probably already be dead."

"He's a marksman?"

"Sober, I never seen a better one," the Doc said. "And he knows these mountains better than any man alive. If flushed, you aren't likely to overtake him. He can run like a deer and stalk a man like a puma."

"We'll get him," Chet vowed.

In reply, the Doc said, "But just in case Dane gets the three of you first, I'll take this occasion to say, so long, it's been good to know all of you."

Before any of them could comment, the Doc went back to bed.

CHAPTER NINETEEN

Because the dapple mare was slow and not strong, Ella rode double behind Gabe. Breath trailing from their nostrils in the frigid mountain dawn, they rounded ice-crusted Potter's Lake and rode north. Among them, only Fidel seemed to be in high spirits, which was remarkable since he was the one that had been wounded the night before.

Following Doc's map proved more difficult than expected because the crotchety old goat had not bothered to pencil in ridges, fast streams, or box canyons. Many times during that first long day, they had to patiently backtrack.

That evening the sun went down early, and they made camp in the lee of some tall boulders where the wind would not be able to get at them if it sprang up hard in the night. They built a good campfire close in under the rocks and heated some of Ella's cooked beef on the ends of willow sticks.

Chet and Gabe were quiet, each man lost in his own brooding thoughts, wondering what the new day would bring and if they would find this Dane fella and the two-toed grizzly. And if they did, would they be able to kill the bear and bring its master to trial?

"It's not the bear's fault so much," Ella said, reading their dark thoughts. "Not if what the Doc suspects is true. I mean, if this Dane fella is the man that controls it, then he's the one that ought to be hanged."

"I agree," Chet said. "It's no different than a man who points a gun at someone and pulls the trigger. You don't blame the gun, you blame the man."

They both looked at Gabe and, finally, Ella asked, "And what do you think?"

"I agree with you," Gabe said, "but I suspect that, once a wild animal has killed horses, cattle, sheep, or men, they'll do it again and again because they've found it to be a whole lot easier to bring down than game." Gabe poked at the fire. "So even though I can understand the bear, I don't think we can just run it deeper into the mountains and expect that it won't come back and kill again."

Gabe's grim assessment did nothing to raise their spirits, and after they had all eaten their fill, including Fidel who ate more than Gabe and Chet combined, they rolled up in their blankets and drifted off to sleep.

They were awakened moments before dawn by Fidel's growl. The dog was tied securely, and when Gabe sat up, his hand went to his gun.

"What is it, boy?"

The dog bared its teeth. Gabe's eyes strained to pierce the faint twilight. When the hair suddenly lifted on Fidel's back, Gabe hissed, "Chet, Ella, move!"

He rolled sideways as a bullet screamed into their camp. It had been aimed at Gabe and would have nailed him dead-center if he hadn't anticipated it and jumped to the side.

Gabe fired twice into the gray dawn, not expecting to do anything more than distract their ambusher. Unfortunately, he didn't succeed. Two more rifle shots crashed across the mountainside as both their horses dropped and began kicking in death.

"Son of a bitch!" Chet swore, unleashing three wild shots. Ella jumped up to run to her mare's side, but Gabe managed to tackle her as more bullets swarmed overhead.

"Stay down!" Gabe yelled into her face.

"But our horses!"

"They're finished! Getting yourself killed over them isn't going to change that."

Ella swallowed noisily, her eyes leaking tears, and then they both kept low and squirmed back to the cover of rocks. Fidel was going crazy, lunging at the rope leash around his neck.

"Quiet," Gabe commanded.

Fidel lapsed into silence, and the forest grew very still. Gabe, Chet, and Ella did not dare move for nearly a quarter of an hour until Gabe slowly raised to his feet and went over to the two dead horses. Both animals had been shot in the head which was damned fine shooting by any man's standards.

"Whatever he is firing, it has a hell of a lot more wallop than our .44 caliber Winchesters," Gabe said darkly.

"What kind of a man would shoot down good horses?" Ella demanded.

"A very ruthless one," Gabe answered. "The kind who would never expect or ask for any quarter. He's a hunter and an expert marksman. He's everything that Doc Landrum warned us he'd be—and worse."

"So what do we do now?" Chet asked.

Gabe reloaded his six-gun. "That's your decision. I'm going after the man."

"Then so are we," Ella swore bitterly as she wiped away her tears. "And I for one will not stop until either he's dead or I am."

Gabe went over to his horse. The buckskin had been no prize, but it had been a good animal, always ready to give its best. Sometimes on frosty mornings it had bucked, and it had even been known to cow-kick and bite if you weren't careful, but the gelding had never backed down from any obstacle on the trail that Gabe had pointed it toward.

"Let's get our rifles, saddlebags, and other gear and get moving," he said. "I'm sure that Dane is a good mile or two from here by now."

Gabe shouldered his gear including the heavy buffalo rifle loaned to him by Paxton and started off on foot to take up a killer's trail.

An hour later, Gabe knelt beside a stream and traced a very faint moccasin track on the damp soil. "Here, is where Dane stopped to drink. Look at the size of the man's foot!"

"I can barely see what you're looking at," Ellas said, squinting at the ground.

Gabe placed his own foot in the track and shook his head. "This man is huge and very clever."

Gabe's eyes followed the streambed. "Dane hiked up this stream, and my guess is that he'll have a place in mind where he can get out of it on rocks that will leave no tracks for a good hundred feet."

"Then how can we track him?" Chet asked.

"You and Ella will fan out on both sides of the stream, and I'll wade up the middle looking for signs," Gabe answered. "Sooner or later, Dane has to leave the stream and maybe between the three of us, we can pick up his trail again."

Chet and Ella exchanged worried glances because they did not share Gabe's keen eye. It was all they could do to see the print that Gabe had just found.

"What if we miss it?" Chet said, voicing their major concern.

Gabe unfolded Doc's map and studied it before he answered. "Then we just keep hiking northwest. If this man has been living up in this part of the woods, he can't hide all of his tracks or the unusual tracks of the two-toed grizzly."

"I just hope," Chet said, "that we find them before they find us. I get the feeling that we might be walking into a trap."

Gabe folded the map and put it back in his pocket. He shared the same concern, but there was little to be gained by admitting the fact. The thing of it was, this was Dane's country. The man would know every square mile of this mountain country and how to use it to his personal advantage.

Chet and Ella again exchanged worried glances prompting Gabe to add, "It's still not too late for the pair of you to return to Potter's Lake."

"I won't quit," Ella said.

"And neither will I," Chet added.

Gabe was secretly pleased. Sure, they were green when it came to tracking and living in the forest, but they were also brave. He knew they'd stand and fight when the right time came.

"Suit yourselves," Gabe told them, as he took Fidel's leash and started up the stream, his eyes studying every rock in search of the one disturbed or overturned.

CHAPTER TWENTY

After Long Rider, Chet, and Ella had left his cabin, Doc Landrum and Sarah had spent a very disagreeable morning dragging the bodies of Caleb Burr's gunmen into a shallow draw. The real work had begun as he'd laboriously covered the bodies with dirt and several tons of rock.

Sweating from his exertions in the cold morning air, Doc had bowed his head and tried to think of something good to say about the murdering hyenas that he'd just buried.

"Lord, they wasn't much, but they were made in the image of Your son, Jesus Christ. And since no one is born bad, I suppose charity of the heart demands that we excuse their degeneracies on a misspent youth without benefit of Your word or a good mother's direction. So, I do hereby commend these blood-thirsty lost souls to the fires of hell, if it is Your will. Amen."

By the time Doc Landrum was finished making his prayer, he was so weary that he barely possessed the strength to trudge back to his cabin. Satisfied that the bodies were protected from wild animals who would not be able to uncover and devour them and that he had spoken fairly to the Lord in behalf of the deceased, the Doc took a long afternoon nap.

That night, even Sarah acted especially tired so Doc stabled her in the little lean-to behind his cabin and fed her well. Sarah made him miss his own old mule who'd passed on in September. He went to bed wondering if Gabe was going to be able to find and capture Dane and kill the two-toed grizzly before it killed anyone else in los Osos Valley. In Doc's opinion, it was highly likely that he'd never see Long Rider, Ella, or Chet Dodson again.

Doc slept very well that night and much later into the morning than usual. The sun was full up when Doc finally rolled out of bed, protesting his sore muscles. Dressed in red woolen long johns, he staggered to the door, threw it open, and knuckled the sleep from his eyes as he waddled out into the yard and spread his feet, preparing to take a leisurely piss.

He was just starting to pass water when a voice behind him graveled, "Mister, turn around real slow and easy."

Doc's flow of water stopped like a bottle just corked. He slipped himself back into his long johns and revolved around to see two men facing him.

"Who the hell are you?"

"Names aren't important," the taller, knife-scarred one said. "The only thing that's important to us is where we can find Long Rider, the Porter woman, and Chet Dodson."

Doc's lower lip curled with contempt. "How the hell should I know? Now get out of my sight, the both of you!"

Horn reached for the bowie knife at his side. "If you don't cooperate and tell us where we can find them, I'm going to cut off your shriveled up old fingers and feed them to you."

Doc Landrum felt his heart begin to thump inside his chest cavity. He did not know these two ornery-looking bastards, but he'd seen their type too many times to kid himself into thinking that they were bluffing. He told himself that he was going to die if he did not play his cards very carefully during the next few moments.

"Maybe we ought to go inside and have some coffee," Doc said, "and talk things over peaceable. I bet you boys are right hungry."

Dooley and Horn both smiled, and Horn said, "Coffee and a hot breakfast would suit us right down to the ground. But first, we want answers."

The Doc shrugged, the picture of innocence. "Mister, I'm afraid I just don't know what you're talking about."

"Is that right?" Dooley asked softly as he advanced, pulling out his six-gun and then jamming it into Doc's protruding belly.

"That's right," Doc heard himself say.

Dooley cocked the hammer back on his gun. "We saw tracks and know that men came here to find them. Now, where the hell did everyone go?"

"I . . . I was off hunting in the woods," Doc said. "When I returned, I also saw tracks. I figured men came by but . . ."

Dooley pistol-whipped him across the side of the head. Doc grunted with pain, then sank to his knees, feeling the cold steel of Dooley's gun barrel being pressed hard to his forehead.

"One last time," Dooley hissed. "Where are they?"

"Go to hell!" Doc Landrum choked.

"Mister," Dooley said, "you're about to go there first."

"Hold up there!" Horn said, pushing between Dooley and Doc. "Maybe we aren't asking the right questions."

Dooley swung on his partner. "What the hell other questions do we need to ask?"

Horn reached down and yanked Doc to his feet. "What I'm wondering about is *why* Long Rider and the others came up here. If they wanted to just run for their lives, they'd have headed for Santa Fe or Denver. You tell me that much, and maybe you'll win your own life."

"Let go of me," Doc said.

Horn let him loose but raised his bowie knife up before Doc's eyes. "I'm not a man to be trifled with so I'll have my answer."

"They're hunting the killer grizzly," Landrum confessed, knowing that this man was going to slit his throat if he told anything but the truth.

Horn shook his head and placed his blade at Doc's gullet. "With a bounty on their heads and men on their heels, do you expect me to believe that?"

"If they find the grizzly, they find the man who uses it to kill, and then they have what they need to bring your boss down."

Horn retracted his knife. "What the hell are you talking about?"

Doc told him about Dane and the two-toed grizzly. When he was finished, both Horn and Dooley were staring at him wide-eyed with astonishment.

Horn said, "I never heard of such a thing as a bear trained to kill!"

"Neither have I," Dooley said. "I think we ought to kill this lying son of a bitch and have some breakfast."

"Now wait a minute," the Doc said, stepping back and raising his hands so they'd listen. "Training a killer bear shouldn't seem so impossible to us. I'm an educated man. I've read a lot, and I know for a fact that the Egyptians trained wild jungle cats and that the Indians have trained wolves. So why couldn't a man train a grizzly bear?"

Horn frowned and shook his head. "Well, when you put it that way, maybe it does make sense."

"Of course it does!" Doc said with relief. "And if you work for Caleb Burr, you must know what kind of a twisted mind he possesses. Using a grizzly to drive terror into the hearts of his enemies would suit his style."

Dooley holstered his pistol and a worried look came into his eyes. "Say, Horn, you expect that was how Mace got his?"

"It's highly possible," Horn said, slipping his knife back into its sheath. "And that does sort of put a new light on things, doesn't it?"

"You got that right," Dooley answered. "But what difference does it make about what we do with this old bird?"

Horn stared into Doc's eyes. "Do you know where this Dane and his pet grizzly are hiding?"

"I might."

"Then you'll take us to find them, Long Rider, and his two friends. I guess I don't have to tell you what will happen if you refuse."

"No," Doc said, "I think I can guess."

"Good," Horn said. "You fix us some breakfast, and we'll leave right after. Try any tricks and we'll kill you on the spot. Understood?"

Doc nodded, and then he was shoved back into the cabin, his mind working furiously to discover some means of getting ahold of a weapon to kill these men before they threw him on Dodson's mule to hurry north toward Dane's secret box canyon.

CHAPTER TWENTY-ONE

"There!" Gabe whispered as he flattened himself against the trunk of a pine causing Ella and Chet to do the same. "Do you see him?"

They followed Gabe's eyes but, already, the huge mountain man was gone.

Gabe jumped out from behind the tree. "I'm taking the dog and going after him. You follow as best you can and don't let him see you. If I can't do the job, it'll be up to you."

Chet nodded. There was no use in pretending that either he or Ella could keep up with Long Rider and the dog that was lunging at the end of its rope leash.

With the buffalo rifle in his right hand and Fidel's leash clenched in his left hand, Gabe took off running after the man that he'd been tracking, knowing that a showdown was at hand. Dane was just a few hundred yards up the mountainside running for his life. Gabe's long legs took him swiftly ahead and Fidel was helping to propel him forward. Scrambling up the mountainside, they came to a swift stream and both man and dog sailed over it without missing stride.

A rifle opened fire and Gabe threw himself on the dog, pulling it down into the pine needles and holding it until he could unholster his six-gun and search for a target. But the target was already off and running again so Gabe jumped to his feet and the chase continued.

His lungs felt as if they were on fire by the time he flattened against a ridge. Caution saved his life because the moment he peered over the ridge, a rifle boomed and Gabe heard the bullet whip-crack overhead. He threw his own buffalo rifle to his shoulder and tracked the big man as he turned to run. Gabe raised the barrel a hair and squeezed off a round. Smoke and fire belched from the big-bored rifle. Gabe saw Dane's stride break for a moment, and then the man disappeared into the trees at the far side of a clearing.

Fighting off the impulse to jump up and continue his pursuit, Gabe reloaded and only then did he shout to the dog. "Let's get him!"

They charged across the clearing into the trees. Gabe halted for a moment to see a small pool of fresh blood. Fidel saw it, too, and barked loudly as they plunged deeper into the forest, running full out.

Suddenly Gabe saw the giant up ahead. He was staggering through the pines, obviously wounded but still able to move with considerable speed.

"Hold it!" Gabe shouted.

Dane whirled around. His face was covered with a gray beard and his hair was shoulder length, scraggly and white. His shoulders were massive and his long, powerful legs were enclosed in thick leather breeches, one of which was staining with fresh blood. Dane raised his rifle, and Gabe jerked Fidel aside as another bullet whistled past them.

"Come and get me!" the giant cried in a voice that sounded as if it came from the depths of a great cavern. "Come and get me!"

Gabe threw the rifle to his shoulder, hoping for a shot, but Dane vanished like smoke in the wind.

"Let's do what the man asks," Gabe said between clenched teeth as he sprang into a run that carried him over yet another ridge and down through a narrow canyon where sheer rock walls pinched in tight until there was no escape.

Over his labored breathing, Gabe suddenly heard a grizzly bear roar in pain and rage, and his blood ran cold. Suddenly, the grizzly appeared just ahead. It was huge! The bear charged. Gabe released Fidel and punched the buffalo rifle against his shoulder. He held his breath for the count of one thousand one, one thousand two, and then he squeezed the trigger.

Over the boom of his rifle, Gabe heard the grizzly bellow in pain. Its demented charge momentarily faltered under the heavy impact of Gabe's bullet and its giant paws slapped at its chest as if had been stung by an angry hornet. But as Gabe's hand streaked for his side arm, the grizzly recovered and kept coming.

Fidel was the only thing between Gabe and the jaws of death. The big dog launched itself at the bear's throat and actually managed to knock it off balance as the six-gun in Gabe's fist slammed home round after round into the grizzly's body.

The mortally wounded bear's great paws caught the dog and crushed it to its bloody chest.

"No, damn you!" Gabe shouted as he drew his blade and plunged it into the beast's exposed throat. The bear collapsed with a shudder, spilling Fidel to the blood-soaked earth.

Gabe's eyes stung with tears as he knelt beside the body of his faithful friend. He tried to remind himself that Paxton had said that this dog, like its parents, had been bred to fight the grizzly. And like his parents, Fidel had died the death of a warrior.

"I'll miss you," he whispered.

Gabe was so engulfed in his sadness that it was almost his undoing. At the last moment he looked up to see Dane, rifle upraised over his head, charging forward.

"I'll knock your brains out!" the giant screamed.

Gabe tossed his empty gun aside and staggered erect to meet the charge. Just as Dane swung his rifle, Gabe ducked and stabbed upward with his bloody knife.

"Ahhh!" the giant cried as Gabe's steel buried itself in Dane's gut all the way to the hilt.

With the giant paralyzed at the end of his blade, Gabe's left hand grabbed his right wrist and he heaved upward with all his might, tearing through the man's insides and bringing Dane up on his toes. The giant's eyes bulged. Gabe yanked his knife free, then jumped back as Dane crashed to the thick mat of pine needles and lay choking.

Gabe knelt beside the mountain giant. "Caleb Burr. He paid you and that grizzly to kill the small ranchers and their herds. Didn't he?"

Dane's eyes focused for an instant causing his face to contort with hatred. "I'll . . . kill . . . you," he snarled as he drew his lips back from his teeth.

Gabe shook his head. "How'd you train the bear? Did you—"

"I'll kill . . . you!" Dane screamed. His huge hands reached for Gabe, fingers opening and closing as he was gripped in the spasms of death. Then he lay still.

Gabe returned to Fidel and knelt again by the dog. "I'll tell John Paxton you were a fighter," he promised. "I'll tell him to breed some more just like you."

Losing the dog hurt Gabe even more than losing his buckskin. But as an Oglala, he had been taught to hide his grief inside and to go on with the struggle of life. So, as best he could, he shook off his sadness and then slowly continued the last few hundred yards up the heavily forested

box canyon. Sure enough, he found Dane's log cabin. It was
solidly constructed, one room, stinking and filthy inside.
There were animal traps hanging from the ceiling and the
walls, and there were stacks of cured furs and some that
were not so cured. The giant had built a rock fireplace,
and because the sun was already dying in the west and
the temperature falling, Gabe started a fire, then prowled
around looking for any clues that might explain what kind
of a twisted devil he'd just killed. It took very little time
to locate a small cave in the side of the canyon wall where
Dane had kept the two-toed grizzly.

As shadows fell across the canyon floor heralding the end
of a bloody day, Gabe hurried down the canyon's mouth to
await the arrival of Chet and Ella.

"Hello!" Chet shouted as he stepped into view with his
rifle to his shoulder.

"It's over!" Gabe told them, quickly explaining how
Fidel had saved his life by diverting the grizzly's demented
charge. "I never saw a braver animal than that dog. I was
starting to get used to having him around."

"I'm sorry," Ella whispered, reading the pain and disappointment in Long Rider's eyes.

"Good God Almighty!" Chet cried. "Look at the size of
that grizzly!"

Ella shrank back with revulsion, no doubt thinking about
how it had been this very beast that had killed her husband
and sent icicles of fear through the valley and driven away
so many others.

She turned her attention to Dane's still form. "What
would possess that man to do such a thing?"

"I don't think we'll ever know the answer to that," Gabe
said. "Maybe the only one who does is Caleb Burr, and
he's not likely to freely talk. My guess is that they struck
a deal—money for services."

"But how did this man train that monster bear to kill on command?"

Gabe moved over to the dead bear. "Take a close look at its eyes. See how they're covered with a glaze?"

"That's caused by death," Chet said.

But Gabe shook his head. "No. I saw those eyes when they were alive, and my hunch is that this old fella was blind, or nearly so. Maybe Dane himself somehow trapped and then purposefully blinded the poor creature. At any rate, if the bear were almost blind, it would be dependent on him. I'd guess that Dane went so far as to cover himself with the scent of a bear. That's just a theory, but one I'd stick to until I heard a better explanation."

Chet shook his head. "What you say kind of makes sense, though. He used a Sharps rifle, huh?"

Gabe picked it up and handed it to Chet. "Keep it as a souvenir."

"What I'd like to do is use it to blow a hole through Caleb Burr."

"You've sure got my support on that," Ella said as she turned away from the bodies.

Gabe motioned up the canyon. "Dane has a cabin. Let's drag his body up there. We'll put it in the same little cave where he kept that killer grizzly. Then let's cut us up some bear meat and . . ."

"Absolutely not!" Ella cried in horror. "That creature probably ate my husband and more than one of my former neighbors!"

Gabe knew that he had made a mistake. "Yeah," he said, "when you put it that way, I can see your point. I guess that we'll have some more of that beef I cooked at your place, Ella. It's getting a little smelly, though."

"Smelly or not, I'm, not eating that bear!"

As darkness was falling, Gabe and Chet buried Fidel, then dragged Dane up to the little cave in the side of the canyon wall and filled the entrance with the same boulders that Dane had used to contain the bear.

"This will be something to tell your kids someday," Gabe said.

Chet raised his eyebrows in a question. "Who says I'm ever going to have kids?"

"Well, if you and Ella are going to keep doing what I caught you doing, then I suppose children are the natural outcome. Don't you agree?"

Chet blushed. "I'm damn sorry about that."

"It's all right," Gabe said as they tromped down to Dane's smelly little cabin and prepared to settle in for the night and eat some moldy beefsteak.

That night, a storm hit the high Rocky Mountains and when they awoke in the morning, the snow was still falling and already about three feet deep.

"We'd better get ourselves out of this canyon before we get buried," Gabe said. "If we can get down to Potter Lake, then we'll thaw out and continue on down to the valley. I'm thinking it's time that we finally had that showdown with Caleb Burr."

Chet nodded. "I agree. But just because you almost single-handedly wiped out his bounty hunters don't mean that he's going to just roll over and play dead when we show up."

"Either way, he's a dead man," Gabe said with grim determination.

That morning was spent fashioning snowshoes. It was not difficult for Gabe had learned how from the Oglala. By noon, they were plowing through the fresh snow. Their minds had already left behind the image of Dane and his killer grizzly. In Gabe's pack was the bear's huge and distinctive two-toed paw as visual evidence to everyone in los Osos Valley that the reign of terror was finally past.

"Gabe," Chet warned, "I'm thinking that by now Caleb will have guessed something went wrong up in these high mountains and he'll have that corrupt United States marshal around to back him up."

"It won't change the outcome," Gabe promised. "The fat man is finished, and if the crooked marshal tries to interfere, he'll have to face the consequences."

"I'll back you all the way," Chet vowed.

"So will I," Ella told him.

Gabe nodded because he'd need all the help he could muster. Mesa, Colorado, was bought and paid for by Caleb Burr. It was his town, his sawmill, and his law. But that was all coming to an end, just as soon as the rich man was locked in dead-center on his gun sight.

CHAPTER TWENTY-TWO

Doc Landrum's eyes were weeping from the cold wind and Chet's mule was being damned uncooperative. Not that Doc could blame poor Sarah because the knife-scarred man named Horn and his friend Dooley had been pushing relentlessly to overtake Long Rider, Ella, and Chet. And since they were approaching the box canyon where Dane and his grizzly were located, Doc had a pretty fair idea that everything was going to come to a bloody climax in just the next hour or two.

"Why are you doing this?" Doc asked, trying to distract these killers so that Long Rider, Ella, and Chet would see them before they were spotted and ambushed.

"For the damn money!" Dooley snapped, wiping his runny nose. "Why the hell else?"

Doc sniffled because his own nose was running in the cold. "You boys ought to just turn around and let this deal pass. No good will come of it, I can tell you that much. Dead men can't spend money."

Horn's eyes never stopped tracking across the country before them. He didn't even turn his head when he said, "Doc, how much farther ahead are they?"

"I'm afraid I don't know," Doc said. "You see . . ."

Doc never had a chance to finish his sentence. Horn's fist slammed into the side of his jaw and Doc grunted with pain as he crashed down to the ground. Doc spat a bloody tooth into the snow and tried to get up, but Horn was out of the saddle and his knife was at Doc's neck.

"How far now?" Horn said. "Tell me or I'll slit your mule's throat and then I'll slit your own."

Doc swallowed a mouthful of blood. "About ten more miles you ornery son of a bitch!"

"What's the layout?"

"I don't know."

Horn pressed the knife down a little.

"I swear I don't know!" Doc hollered. "I just came close enough to Dane's canyon to figure out where it was. The man would have killed me if he'd seen me."

"Maybe he already killed Long Rider, the girl, and Dodson," Dooley suggested in a worried voice. "If he did that, we'll have to find their bodies. Burr is gonna be real upset about the girl dying."

But Horn lifted the knife from Doc's neck and shook his head. "Naw. Even if the mountain man did kill Chet and Long Rider—which I doubt—he'd have kept the woman for his own pleasure. A lonesome man like that would be crazy to kill such a good-lookin' woman. He'd keep her at least through the cold of winter."

Dooley nodded. "I guess you're right about that."

Horn remounted. "Doc, get back on that mule and keep your goddamn mouth shut when we spot someone."

Doc climbed on Sarah wishing he was man enough to kill this pair all by himself. Trouble was, he wasn't man enough. Oh, he could shoot straight, but he wasn't anywhere near in the same league with these ruthless hired killers, and he supposed that was to his credit.

It's up to Long Rider and Chet, Doc thought miserably, and they don't even know we're coming.

Two hours later, Gabe was in the lead breaking trail when he rounded the side of a mountain. The wind was blowing hard and cold, but a weak sun had melted the snow away except in the shady places. In other spots, the ground was slick with ice and the footing very treacherous. Gabe was starting to pick the safest trail down when a voice from behind him said, "Anyone moves a muscle, you're all dead."

Gabe froze in his snowshoes. Just behind him, Chet did the same. Only Ella turned to see Horn and Dooley spur their horses out from behind some rocks with Doc and Sarah wedged in between them. The two hired gunmen had their Colts trained on their targets. Poor Doc's head hung with defeat, his lips broken and the lower part of his face smeared with blood. He appeared to have aged twenty years.

Horn said, "Get off that mule and take their guns, Doc. Take 'em out of their holsters real slow and easy. You make one false move, we'll drop you and the rest of them. Caleb's bounty is for dead or alive."

Doc raised his head and when his eyes locked with Ella's, she saw them glint with hatred and determination. Ella knew at a glance that Doc was anything but resigned or defeated.

"Ella," Dooley said, "Caleb wants you brought back to him alive. Get over here and climb on the mule."

She raised her chin. "No."

Dooley's cheeks flushed with anger. He cocked the hammer of his gun and pointed it at the back of Gabe's head. "Woman, get your pretty ass on that mule right now or I'll blow his damn brains out!"

Ella felt her heart sink. Dooley would do exactly as he threatened so she mounted Sarah, her heart hammering against her ribs.

"Doc, hurry up!" Dooley ranted. "We ain't got all winter!"

Chet was the nearest, and Doc slowly eased his six-gun out of his holster. "Steady," Doc whispered, moving toward Gabe.

Gabe felt Doc bump up against him and start to lift his gun out of its holster even as the man slipped Chet's gun into his hand and shouted, "Now!"

Gabe spun around as Dooley and Horn opened fire, their bullets plowing into Doc's thick, shielding body. Gabe's six-gun bucked in his fist. Dooley screamed in pain, then Horn spurred his horse forward. Before Gabe could unleash another round, Horn's mount was knocking him over the side of the mountain. He struck the slope and began to roll, careening wildly down the icy mountain toward a distant river. Chet's gun went flying from Gabe's hand and he felt something sharp snap in his leg.

Dimly, Gabe heard more gunfire and then Horn shout, "Dooley, Long Rider is mine!"

Gabe landed in a pile of brush at the bottom of the canyon and blacked out to the sound of a river and hoofbeats. He wasn't sure how long he was out, but when he roused awake, he looked up to see Horn coming at him with his bowie knife and a cruel smile.

"Mister, shootin' you would be too damn easy. I wanna feel your blood spillin' over my hands."

Gabe's own hand went to *his* knife and found its handle. He pushed himself erect, feeling dizzy and weak. His mind tried to come to bear on what had happened. Were Chet and the Doc still alive? What about Ella?

As if reading Long Rider's frantic and confused thoughts,

Horn chuckled. "Your friend is up on top, a bullet in his belly. He'll die slow. The woman is on her way to Burr's ranch just as sure as you're on your way to hell."

Gabe shook his head. His right leg felt numb, and he wondered if it was broken. He pounded his right foot down on the rocks and pain shot up his leg telling him that, indeed, the leg was broken.

"What's the matter, Long Rider," Horn sneered, "bad wheel?"

"It'll do for the likes of you."

Horn waved his knife to and fro before his shining eyes. "I'm going to carve you up one little piece at a time. Like I do the greasers I've cut down in Old Mexico. The ones that thought they were the best."

"Talk is real cheap," Gabe said, taking a deep breath and lowering himself to a crouch. Given his broken leg, he sure didn't see how he was going to be able to get out of the way of Horn's knife but when it came to knife fighting, sometimes the last man standing was simply the one who most wanted to live.

Horn raised his left arm like a shield and advanced, his bowie knife out in front of him, cutting edge up. He feigned, but Gabe did not buy the ruse.

"Ha! So you have done this before!" Horn cried. "Good! I like it interesting."

"It'll be more than that before we're though," Gabe vowed, glancing behind him to make sure that he was not about to trip over brush or rocks. Fortunately, they were standing in a small circular clearing about twenty feet across.

Horn feigned twice more and each time Gabe stayed in a good knife-fighting position, blade up and slightly forward, right leg planted just ahead of his left, very much in the fighting posture of a fencer.

"Come on!" Horn snarled. "Come and fight!"

But Gabe just smiled. He had seen many more knife fights than he'd fought and had a hunch that patience was a great advantage so he waited.

Horn lost his patience. With the hiss of a snake, he lunged again, only this time his knife drove straight for Gabe's face. Gabe ducked, his arm shot out, and his blade entered Horn's body just below his outstretched arm.

The killer screamed and when he attempted to pull back, Gabe's left hand grabbed him by the coat and slung him down. Gabe's knees landed on Horn's right wrist, pinning his knife in the snow and then Gabe plunged his knife into the man's body just below the point where his ribs met.

Horn's mouth formed a circle and a silent scream formed on his bloodless lips. Gabe yanked his knife free and rolled away.

"You lose this time," Gabe whispered as he pushed himself erect and then began to scramble as fast as he could up the steep, icy mountainside.

CHAPTER TWENTY-THREE

Gabe ripped open Chet's coat and shirt saying, "You're about as lucky as a man can get. Your belt buckle took the bullet's impact and when it ricocheted into your gut, it didn't do much more than give you a second belly button."

"I knew that I was a goner if I opened my eyes," Chet whispered as he crawled to his feet. "But goddamn them, look what they done to poor old Doc!"

Tears were streaking down Chet's cheeks as Gabe hobbled over to kneel beside Doc. The man had taken two bullets in the back as he'd purposefully shielded Gabe and saved his life.

"He must have liked me to have done that," Gabe said with a sad shake of his head.

"Yeah," Chet answered, "I could tell that he did. A couple of times, Doc ask me about your Indian upbringing and stuff like that. He said you were a good man and the kind of friend he'd never found to trust in a bad scrape."

Gabe pushed himself erect. "We got to bury him or the wolves will take care of him before we can return."

"I know," Chet said, "but the trouble is, we don't have much time because there's no telling what Caleb Burr will do to Ella."

"Then let's find some sticks and start digging."

But when Gabe tried to hobble away, Chet exclaimed, "Why, you've got a broken leg!"

"Yeah," Gabe said, glancing down at the leg and then hobbling over to embrace the trunk of a scrubby, wind-blown pine, "and you're going to have to grab hold of my foot and set it."

Chet started to protest until he saw the iron resolution on Gabe's face. Taking a deep breath, Chet clamped his hands on Gabe's right boot and lifted it very gently. "I never did anything like this before. I could cripple you permanently."

"That's a chance we have to take," Gabe said, beads of sweat popping out across his forehead. "So just pull it straight, fast and hard."

Chet swallowed noisily and then he jerked the boot. Gabe bit back a cry of pain and almost passed out.

"You all right?" Chet cried, jumping to his side.

"Yeah." Gabe discovered he was breathing rapidly as he traced his fingertips down his pants leg. "But it felt as if you were bound and determined to tear my leg from its socket."

"You said to pull hard."

"True enough," Gabe said between clenched teeth, "and the leg bone is straight again. All we have to do is splint it up, get Doc buried, and get out of these high mountains before another snowstorm hits."

"And somehow rescue Ella and kill Caleb Burr," Chet added.

"That's right. So let's not waste any more time shootin' the breeze."

Somehow, they did get the Doc buried and made it off the mountain. They tracked Ella and an obviously wounded

B. D. Dooley to Potter's Lake and then fought a blizzard for seven hours to reach Caleb Burr's ranch late in the night and by then, Long Rider's leg was throbbing like a Cheyenne drum.

"Look!" Gabe said.

They both stared into the bed of an unhitched wagon to see a snow-covered shroud. Gabe hobbled over to the wagon, reached inside, and pulled the stiff canvas shroud away to see Dooley's frozen, staring face.

Chet took an involuntary back step. "You think you mortally wounded him up on the mountain, or did Burr kill him?"

"Does it matter?"

Chet shook his head and gazed back through the swirling snow toward the dark, silent ranch house. There was no visible light in the windows, and Gabe's biggest fear was that they might kill Ella or other innocent people in a night gun battle.

"I don't suppose you have any idea where Burr sleeps," Gabe said through frozen, cupped hands held against the wind.

"No."

"Then let's find him if we have to search every room in the place," Gabe said, figuring that no one would be guarding against an attack on such a bitter night.

They entered the ranch house where candles faintly illuminated every room and hallway. Gabe, hobbling painfully, led Chet down a hallway that looked promising. When he came to the first door, he eased it open and peered inside. The room was totally dark, but he could hear someone's breathing so he stepped back into the hallway.

"Get me that candle."

When Chet handed it to him, Gabe moved back inside the room, trying to be as quiet as possible. As he drew nearer, he saw the shapely curve of a woman's body under blankets and that sent him rushing forward.

"Ella!" he whispered.

But it *wasn't* Ella. This one reeked of cheap whiskey and when her bloodshot eyes flew open, she screamed into Gabe's face.

"Hush!" Gabe ordered. "All I want to know is where I can find Caleb Burr!"

For a moment, Lulu stared at him, dumb with incomprehension, then her booze-bloated face twisted with hatred. "Two doors down. Kill him! Hear me? You kill that fat, cheating son of a bitch!"

"Lady," Gabe said, shoving the woman away with revulsion, "right now, that's my whole purpose."

Just as Gabe reached the hallway again, he heard a shout and then a scream. Ella came racing down the hallway, and even in the candlelight Gabe could see that her face was swollen and bruised. She threw herself into Chet's arms. An instant later, Caleb stumbled into the hallway but when he saw Gabe, he started to twist around and dart back into his room.

"Freeze or you're a dead man!" Gabe shouted, his gun coming up.

Caleb froze. Then, very slowly, he turned, his body almost filling the width of the hallway, his deep-set little eyes moving like those of a cornered rat.

"Well, now," he breathed, "what do we have here? Thieves in my house? Friend, I'm afraid that you have broken the law. It just so happens that Marshal Flowers is here as my guest, and he'll have to arrest you and send you and poor Chet away for a long, long time."

"He can try," Gabe growled.

"Kill him!" Lulu shrieked, jumping between them. "Caleb deserves to die. Shoot him!"

Gabe wanted to, but it was not in him to gun down a helpless man. Not even an animal like Caleb Burr. "Chet, toss your gun at his feet."

"What?"

"Do it!" Gabe ordered.

But Caleb shook his head, chins wagging. "Oh no," he said, "I'm not going to do that. Not against a man like you!"

"Toss him your gun," Gabe repeated through clenched teeth. "That gives him a fighting chance and the right to choose how he wants to die."

"Marshal!" Caleb shouted, looking up the hallway and seeing no help in sight. "Goodamnit, Marshal, come and help me!"

Chet tossed his gun, but the throw was short and just as Gabe was deciding to kick the gun closer to the fat man, he felt a terrible blow strike him behind the ear. His legs buckled and he sank to the carpet as his gun was wrenched out of his hand.

"Bastard!" Lulu screamed as she cocked back the hammer of Gabe's Colt and opened fire.

Gabe looked up to see Caleb stagger, then raise his hands before himself as if he could ward off bullets. Lulu's second shot ripped a hole through his palm before it struck the fat man in the mouth.

Gabe didn't want to watch anymore as a third bullet sent the huge, quivering body staggering backward down the hallway. Caleb crashed to the floor, but the gun in Lulu's hand kept firing until it was empty. Then she hurled it at the body.

Smoke hung heavily in the hallway and suddenly, they heard the pounding of bare feet. Gabe scooped up Chet's six-gun an instant before a man clad in a red flannel nightshirt plowed around a corner with a gun in his own hand.

"What the hell is going on here?"

"Who are you to ask?" Gabe demanded, his barrel trained on the man's breastbone.

"I'm United States Marshal Dwight Flowers. Who shot Mr. Burr?"

Ella reacted quickest. "Marshal, Caleb Burr just committed suicide. There's his gun. Take a look for yourself."

Flowers' eyes took in everything at a glance, and he waved the gun at all of them. "That's nonsense! Now I repeat—which one of you killed Mr. Burr?"

Gabe kept his gun trained on Flowers. He did not think the marshal had much sand, but he was not taking any chances. "Ella just told you, Marshal. Burr went crazy and shot himself to death. We'll all swear to that."

The marshal shoved past them and snatched up Gabe's empty pistol lying beside the bullet-riddled body. "And you expect me to believe Mr. Burr shot himself *six times*?"

Gabe shrugged.

Lulu raised her head. "Caleb was a strong man, and he took a lot of killing. I ought to know."

"Lulu, if—"

Gabe reached out, grabbed the marshal, and slammed him up against the hallway. "Mister, I've been fighting your kind of corrupt officials my whole life. So make up your mind right now. Walk away from a suicide or join Caleb Burr in a short walk to hell."

Flowers' mouth worked silently. He studied Gabe's eyes and then he glanced at Ella, Chet, and Lulu. "Well . . . well if you all saw Mr. Burr shoot himself, that's that, I reckon!"

Gabe released the man. "Get the hell out our sight."

Flowers tried to muster up some semblance of dignity, but it was hopeless in his nightshirt and bare feet. So he just turned and rushed back to his bedroom.

Ella threw her arms around Chet's neck and hugged him tightly. The rancher held his woman and said to Gabe, "It might take a little time, but Ella is going to be all right. This valley is going to be all right now."

"I know that," Gabe said quietly. He picked up his empty gun and reloaded it.

"Tell me the truth," Chet said, "would you really have gunned down the marshal?"

"Damn right I would have. I'm never going to be locked in a cell again for something I didn't do wrong."

"What about me?" Lulu asked.

"Go back to bed, Miss. Your nightmare is over."

"Will you take me out of here?" she asked Gabe in a trembling voice. "I just want out."

"If you sober up, I will take you from this valley. Santa Fe isn't too far and it's a sight warmer."

Lulu sniffled. "Then that's where I'll go with you."

"Good," Long Rider said as he turned away and went looking for a clean, dry bed for sleeping.

Special Preview!

Award-winning author Bill Gulick presents his epic
trilogy of the American West, the magnificent story of
two brothers, Indian and white man, bound by blood
and divided by destiny . . .

NORTHWEST DESTINY

This classic saga includes *Distant Trails*, *Gathering
Storm*, and *River's End*.

*Following is a special excerpt from Book One,
DISTANT TRAILS—available from Jove Books . . .*

For the last hundred yards of the stalk, neither man had spoke—not even in whispers—but communicated by signs as they always did when hunting meat to fill hungry bellies. Two steps ahead, George Drewyer, the man recognized to be the best hunter in the Lewis and Clark party, sank down on his right knee, froze, and peered intently through the glistening wet bushes and dangling evergreen tree limbs toward the animal grazing in the clearing. Identifying it, he turned, using his hands swiftly and graphically to tell the younger, less experienced hunter, Matt Crane, the nature of the animal he had seen and how he meant to approach and kill it.

Not a deer, his hands said. Not an elk. Just a stray Indian horse—with no Indians in sight. He'd move up on it from downwind, his hands said, until he got into sure-kill range, then he'd put a ball from his long rifle into its head. What he expected Matt to do was follow a couple of steps behind and a few feet off to the right, stopping when he stopped, aiming when he aimed, but firing only if the actions of the horse clearly showed that Drewyer's ball had missed.

Matt signed that he understood. Turning back toward the clearing, George Drewyer began his final stalk.

Underfoot, the leaf mold and fallen pine needles formed a yielding carpet beneath the scattered clumps of bushes and thick stands of pines, which here on the western slope of the Bitter Root Mountains were broader in girth and taller than the skinny lodgepole and larch found on the higher reaches of the Lolo Trail. Half a day's travel behind, the other thirty-two members of the party still were struggling in foot-deep snow over slick rocks, steep slides, and tangles of down timber treacherous as logjams, as they sought the headwaters of the Columbia and the final segment of their journey to the Pacific Ocean.

It had been four days since the men had eaten meat. Matt knew, being forced to sustain themselves on the detested army ration called "portable soup," a grayish brown jelly that looked like a mixture of pulverized wood duff and dried dung, tasted like iron filings, and even when flavored with meat drippings and dissolved in hot water satisfied the belly no more than a swallow of air. Nor had the last solid food been much, for the foal butchered at Colt-Killed Creek had been dropped by its dam only a few months ago; though its meat was tender enough, most of its growth had gone into muscle and bone, its immature carcass making skimpy portions when distributed among such a large party of famished men.

With September only half gone, winter had already come to the seven-thousand-foot-high backbone of the continent a week's travel behind. All the game that the old Shoshone guide, Toby, had told them usually was to be found in the high meadows at this time of year had moved down to lower levels. Desperate for food, Captain William Clark had sent George Drewyer and Matt Crane scouting ahead for meat, judging that two men travelling afoot and unencumbered would stand a much better chance of finding game than the main party with its thirty-odd men and twenty-nine heavily laden horses. As he usually did, Drewyer had found game of a sort, weighed the risk of rousing the hostility of its Indian owner against the need of the party for food, and decided that hunger recognized no property rights.

In the drizzling cold rain, the coat of the grazing horse glistened like polished metal. It would be around four years old, Matt guessed, a brown and white paint, well muscled, sleek, alert. If this were a typical Nez Perce horse, he could well believe what the Shoshone chief, Cameahwait, had told Captain Clark—that the finest horses to be found in this part of the country were those raised by the Shoshones' mortal enemies, the Nez Perces. Viewing such a handsome animal cropping bluegrass on a Missouri hillside eighteen months ago, Matt Crane would have itched to rope, saddle, and ride it, testing its speed, wind, and spirit. Now all he itched to do was kill and eat it.

Twenty paces away from the horse, which still was grazing placidly, George Drewyer stopped, knelt behind a fallen tree, soundlessly rested the barrel of his long rifle on its trunk, and took careful aim. Two steps to his right, Matt Crane did the same. After what seemed an agonizingly long period of time, during which Matt held his breath, Drewyer's rifle barked. Without movement or sound, the paint horse sank to the ground, dead—Matt was sure—before its body touched the sodden earth.

"Watch it!" Drewyer murmured, swiftly reversing his rifle, swabbing out its barrel with the ramrod, expertly reloading it with patched and greased lead ball, wiping flint and firing hammer clean, then opening the pan and pouring in a carefully measured charge while he protected it from the drizzle with the tree trunk and his body.

Keeping his own rifle sighted on the fallen horse, Matt held his position without moving or speaking, as George Drewyer had taught him to do, until the swarthy, dark-eyed hunter had reloaded his weapon and risen to one knee. Peering first at the still animal, then moving his searching gaze around the clearing, Drewyer tested the immediate environment with all his senses—sight, sound, smell, and his innate hunter's instinct—for a full minute before he at last nodded in satisfaction.

"A bunch-quitter, likely. Least there's no herd nor herders around. Think you can skin it, preacher boy?"

"Sure. You want it quartered, with the innards saved in the hide?"

"Just like we'd do with an elk. Save everything but the hoofs and whinny. Get at it, while I snoop around for Injun sign. The Nez Perces will be friendly, the captains say, but I'd as soon not meet the Injun that owned that horse till its head and hide are out of sight."

While George Drewyer circled the clearing and prowled through the timber beyond, Matt Crane went to the dead horse, unsheathed his butcher knife, skillfully made the cuts needed to strip off the hide, and gutted and dissected the animal. Returning from his scout, Drewyer hunkered down beside him, quickly boned out as large a packet of choice cuts as he could conveniently carry, wrapped them in a piece of hide, and loaded the still-warm meat into the empty canvas backpack he had brought along for that purpose.

"It ain't likely the men'll get this far by dark," he said, "so I'll take 'em a taste to ease their bellies for the night. Can you make out alone till tomorrow noon?"

"Yes."

"From what I seen, the timber thins out a mile or so ahead. Seems to be a kind of open, marshy prairie beyond, which is where the Nez Perces come this time of year to dig roots, Toby says. Drag the head and hide back in the bushes out of sight. Cut the meat up into pieces you can spit and broil, then build a fire and start it cooking. If the smoke and smell brings Injun company, give 'em the peace sign, invite 'em to sit and eat, and tell 'em a big party of white men will be coming down the trail tomorrow. You got all that, preacher boy?"

"Yes."

"Good. Give me a hand with this pack and I'll be on my way." Slipping his arms through the straps and securing the pad that transferred a portion of the weight to his forehead, Drewyer got to his feet while Matt Crane eased the load. Grinning, Drewyer squeezed his shoulder. "Remind me to quit calling you preacher boy, will you, Matt? You've learned a lot since you left home."

"I've had a good teacher."

"That you have! Take care."

Left alone in the whispering silence of the forest and the cold, mist-like rain, Matt Crane dragged the severed head and hide into a clump of nearby bushes. Taking his hatchet, he searched for and found enough resinous wood, bark, and dry duff to catch the spark from his flint and steel. As the fire grew in the narrow trench he had dug for it, he cut forked sticks, placed pieces of green aspen limbs horizontally across them, sliced the meat into strips, and started it to broiling. The smell of juice dripping into the fire made his belly churn with hunger, tempting him to do what Touissant Charbonneau, the party's French-Canadian interpreter, did when fresh-killed game was brought into camp—seize a hunk and gobble it down hot, raw, and bloody. But he did not, preferring to endure the piercing hunger pangs just a little longer in exchange for the greater pleasure of savoring his first bite of well-cooked meat.

Cutting more wood for the fire, he hoped George Drewyer would stop calling him "preacher boy." Since at twenty he was one of the youngest members of the party and his father, the Reverend Peter Crane, was a Presbyterian minister in St. Louis, it had been natural enough for the older men to call him "the preacher's boy" at first. Among a less disciplined band, he would have been forced to endure a good deal of hoorawing and would have been the butt of many practical jokes. But the no-nonsense military leadership of the two captains put strict limits on that sort of thing.

Why Drewyer—who'd been raised a Catholic, could barely read and write, and had no peer as an outdoorsman—should have made Matt his protégé, Matt himself could not guess. Maybe because he was malleable, did what he was told to do, and never backed off from hard work. Maybe because he listened more than he talked. Or maybe because he was having the adventure of his life and showed it. Whatever the reason, their relationship was good. It would be even better, Matt mused, if Drewyer would drop the "preacher boy" thing and simply call him by name.

While butchering the horse, Matt noticed that it had been gelded as a colt. According to George Drewyer, the Nez Perces were one of the few Western Indian tribes that practiced selective breeding, thus the high quality of their horses. From the way Chief Cameahwait had acted, a state of war existed between the Shoshones and the Nez Perces, so the first contact between the Lewis and Clark party— which had passed through Shoshone country—and the Nez Perces was going to be fraught with danger. Aware of the fact that he might make the first contact, Matt Crane felt both uneasy and proud. Leaving him alone in this area showed the confidence Drewyer had in him. But his aloneness made him feel a little spooky.

With the afternoon only half gone and nothing to do but tend the fire, Matt stashed his blanket roll under a tree out of the wet, picked up his rifle, and curiously studied the surrounding forest. There was no discernible wind, but vagrant currents of air stirred, bringing to his nostrils the smell of wood smoke, of crushed pine needles, of damp leaf mold, of burnt black powder. As he moved across the clearing toward a three-foot-wide stream gurgling down the slope, he scowled, suddenly realizing that the burnt black powder smell could not have lingered behind this long. Nor would it have gotten stronger, as this smell was doing the nearer he came to the stream. Now he identified it beyond question.

Sulfur! There must be a mineral-impregnated hot spring nearby, similar to the hot springs near Traveler's Rest at the eastern foot of Lolo Pass, where the cold, weary members of the party had eased their aches and pains in warm, soothing pools. What he wouldn't give for a hot bath right now!

At the edge of the stream, he knelt, dipping his hand into the water. It was warm. Cupping his palm, he tasted it, finding it strongly sulfurous. If this were like the stream on the other side of the mountains, he mused, there would be one or more scalding, heavily impregnated springs issuing from old volcanic rocks higher up the slope, their waters diluted by colder side rivulets joining the main stream, making it simply a matter of exploration to find water temperature and a chemical content best suited to the needs of a cold, tired body. The prospect intrigued him.

Visually checking the meat broiling over the fire, he judged it could do without tending for an hour or so. Thick though the forest cover was along the sides of the stream, he would run no risk of getting lost, for following the stream downhill would bring him back to the clearing.

Time enough then to cut limbs for a lean-to and rig a shelter
for the night.

Sometimes wading in the increasingly warm waters of the
stream, sometimes on its bush-bordered bank, he followed
its windings uphill for half a mile before he found what
he was looking for: a pool ten feet long and half as wide,
eroded in smooth basalt, ranging in depth from one to four
feet. Testing the temperature of its water, he found it just
right—hot but not unbearably so, the sulfur smell strong
but not unpleasant. Leaning his rifle against a tree trunk,
he took off his limp, shapeless red felt hat, pulled his thin
moccasins off his bruised and swollen feet, waded into the
pool, and gasped with sensual pleasure as the heat of the
water spread upwards.

Since his fringed buckskin jacket and woolen trousers
already were soaking wet from the cold rain, he kept them
on as he first sank to a sitting position, then stretched
out full length on his back, with only his head above
water. After a time, he roused himself long enough to strip
the jacket off over his head and pull the trousers down
over his ankles. Tossing them into a clump of bushes near
his rifle, hat, and moccasins, he lay back in the soothing
water, naked, warm, and comfortable for the first time since
Traveler's Rest.

Drowsily, his eyes closed. He slept . . .

The sound that awakened him some time later could have
been made by a deer moving down to drink from the pool
just upstream from where he lay. It could have been made
by a beaver searching for a choice willow sapling to cut
down. It could have been made by a bobcat, a bear, or
a cougar. But as consciousness returned to him, as he
heard the sound and attempted to identify it, his intelligence
rejected each possibility that occurred to him the moment it

crossed his mind—for one lucid reason.

Animals did not sing. And whatever this intruder into his state of tranquillity might be, it was singing.

Though the words were not recognizable, they had an Indian sound, unmistakably conveying the message that the singer was at peace with the world, not self-conscious, and about to indulge in a very enjoyable act. Turning over on his belly, Matt crawled to the upper end of the pool, peering through the screening bushes in the direction from which the singing sound was coming. The light was poor. Even so, it was good enough for him to make out the figure of a girl, standing in profile not ten feet away, reaching down to the hem of her buckskin skirt, lifting it, and pulling it over her head.

As she tossed the garment aside, she turned, momentarily facing him. His first thought was *My God, she's beautiful!* His second: *She's naked!* His third, *How can I get away from here without being seen?*

That she was not aware of his presence was made clear enough by the fact that she still was crooning her bath-taking song, her gaze intent on her footing as she stepped gingerly into a pool just a few yards upstream from the one in which he lay. Though he had stopped breathing for fear she would hear the sound, he could not justify leaving his eyes open for fear she would hear the lids closing. Morally wrong though he knew it was to stare at her, he could not even blink or look away.

She would be around sixteen years old, he judged, her skin light copper in color, her mouth wide and generous, with dimples indenting both cheeks. Her breasts were full but not heavy; her waist was slim, her stomach softly rounded, her hips beginning to broaden with maturity, her legs long and graceful. Watching her sink slowly into the water until only the tips of her breasts and her head were

exposed, Matt felt no guilt for continuing to stare at her.
Instead he mused, *So that's what a naked woman looks like!
Why should I be ashamed to admire such beauty?*

He began breathing again, careful to make no sound.
Since the two pools were no more than a dozen feet apart,
separated by a thin screen of bushes and a short length of
stream, which here made only a faint gurgling noise, he
knew that getting out of the water, retrieving his clothes
and rifle, and then withdrawing from the vicinity without revealing his presence would require utmost caution.
But the attempt must be made, for if one young Indian
woman knew of this bathing spot, others must know of
it, too, and in all likelihood soon would be coming here
to join her.

He could well imagine his treatment at their hands, if
found. Time and again recently the two captains had warned
members of the party that Western Indians such as the
Shoshones, Flatheads, and Nez Perces had a far higher
standard of morality than did the Mandans, with whom
the party had wintered, who would gladly sell the favor
of wives and daughters for a handful of beads, a piece of
bright cloth, or a cheap trade knife, and cheerfully provide
shelter and bed for the act.

Moving with infinite care, he half floated, half crawled
to the lower right-hand edge of the pool, where he had left
his rifle and clothes. The Indian girl was still singing. The
bank was steep and slick. Standing up, he took hold of a
sturdy-feeling, thumb-thick sapling rooted near the edge of
the bank, cautiously tested it, and judged it secure. Pulling
himself out of the pool, he started to take a step, slipped,
and tried to save himself by grabbing the sapling with both
hands.

The full weight of his body proved too much for its root
system. Torn out of the wet earth, it no longer supported

him. As he fell backward into the pool, he gave an involuntary cry of disgust.

"Oh, shit!"

Underwater, his mouth, nose, and eyes filled as he struggled to turn over and regain his footing. When he did so, he immediately became aware of the fact that the girl had stopped singing. Choking, coughing up water, half-blinded, and completely disoriented, he floundered out of the pool toward where he thought his clothes and rifle were. Seeing a garment draped over a bush, he grabbed it, realized it was not his, hastily turned away, and blundered squarely into a wet, naked body.

To save themselves from falling, both he and the Indian girl clung to each other momentarily. She began screaming. Hastily he let her go. Still screaming and staring at him with terror-stricken eyes, she snatched the dress off the bush and held it so that it covered her. Finding his own clothes, he held them in front of his body, trying to calm the girl by making the sign for "friend," "white man," and "peace," while urgently saying:

"*Ta-ba-bone,* you understand? *Suyapo!* I went to sleep, you see, and had no idea you were around . . ."

Suddenly her screaming stopped. Not because of his words or hand signs, Matt feared, but because of the appearance of an Indian man who had pushed through the bushes and now stood beside her. He was dressed in beaded, fringed buckskins, was stocky, slightly bowlegged, a few inches shorter than Matt but more muscular and heavier, a man in his middle twenties, with high cheekbones and a firm jawline. He shot a guttural question at the girl, to which she replied in a rapid babble of words. His dark brown eyes blazed with anger. Drawing a glittering knife out of its sheath, he motioned the girl to step aside, and moved toward Matt menacingly.

Backing away, Matt thought frantically, *Captain Clark is not going to like this at all. And if that Indian does what it looks like he means to do with that knife, I'm not going to like it, either . . .*